*

TWICE

Cormac gave Skye Fargo no warning before the rifle exploded, the boom echoing off the rocks around them. Fargo stood holding the barrel pointed off to the side. He'd grabbed it the instant Cormac had brought it around.

The Irishman's face was dark with hate, his blond hair glinted in the blood-red sunset. He dropped his rifle, and his fists came up. But before he could make a move, Fargo lashed out, his powerful right driving into the man's belly. Skye followed with a snapping swift uppercut, left fist to the jaw as Cormac's head jerked around with a crunch.

"Had enough?" Fargo asked.

Cormac nodded as if drunk, and Fargo turned away toward the other ranch hands looking on. Too late Skye heard the rustle behind him and half turned as Cormac's knife bit deep into his side. Then the steel blade swept upward, seeking Skye's face, his hands, his throat. He felt it cold and hot, the blood silvery and slick.

It was time to get serious—or get dead. . . .

BE SURE TO READ THE OTHER THRILLING NOVELS IN THE EXCITING *TRAILSMAN* SERIES!

(WR)

BLUE SIERRA RENEGADES

by

Jon Sharpe

A SIGNET BOOK

SIGNET
Published by the Penguin Group
Penguin Books USA Inc., 375 Hudson Street,
New York, New York 10014, U.S.A.
Penguin Books Ltd, 27 Wrights Lane,
London W8 5TZ, England
Penguin Books Australia Ltd, Ringwood,
Victoria, Australia
Penguin Books Canada Ltd, 10 Alcorn Avenue,
Toronto, Ontario, Canada M4V 3B2
Penguin Books (N.Z.) Ltd, 182–190 Wairau Road,
Auckland 10, New Zealand

Penguin Books Ltd, Registered Offices:
Harmondsworth, Middlesex, England

First published by Signet, an imprint of Dutton Signet,
a division of Penguin Books USA Inc.

First Printing, June, 1997
10 9 8 7 6 5 4 3 2

The first chapter of this book originally appeared in *Bullet Hole Claims,*
the one hundred eighty-fifth volume in this series.

The Trailsman

Beginnings . . . they bend the tree and they mark the man. Skye Fargo was born when he was eighteen. Terror was his midwife, vengeance his first cry. Killing spawned Skye Fargo, ruthless, cold-blooded murder. Out of the acrid smoke of gunpowder still hanging in the air, he rose, cried out a promise never forgotten.

The Trailsman they began to call him all across the West: searcher, scout, hunter, the man who could see where others only looked, his skills for hire but not his soul, the man who lived each day to the fullest, yet trailed each tomorrow. Skye Fargo, the Trailsman, and the seeker who could take the wildness of a land and the wanting of a woman and make them his own.

1860, the village of Corazon, Old Mexico,
where the parched mountains are blue as cool water.
Where bitterness and greed simmer
in the heart of every man and every woman . . .

1

It isn't every day a man gets to go to his own funeral.

On that July afternoon, just after the time for siesta, the sun was heading down toward the rim of the barren and almost impassable mountains that surrounded the high desert plain. Slanting light, filtered by dust in the thin air, washed the color of unpolished brass across the rutted road between the adobes that made up the sleepy village of Corazon.

A tall stranger rode slowly into town on a clopping gray. The horse's hooves kicked up small fans of dust. Something about the man made the people of Corazon pause and look. Maybe it was the power of his broad shoulders beneath the tattered wool serape. Or the way his hands held the reins with such assurance. Or the angle of his dark, battered hat, pulled low to hide most of his face so that all that could be seen was a dark bearded chin.

Or maybe they stopped to stare at the black-and-white pinto, with the rare pattern that marked it as an Ovaro. He was leading it behind him. It was a magnificent horse with a deep chest, powerful legs, and splendid head, the kind of horse that once glimpsed, was not easily forgotten. Across the pinto's back lay a dead man tied to the saddle, facedown, his legs and arms dangling. Dead men were a common sight in Corazon. This one was a gringo in jeans and a leather vest. Blood dripped from his head, leaving a dotted trail down the street. A Colt glittered in the dead man's holster. A lot of good it would do him now.

The tall stranger in the serape brought both horses to a halt and dismounted. He stood before the cantina, a large adobe building with a wooden portico surmounted by a thatch of ocotillo branches. He shouted out something, a gringo greeting of some kind. By now, everyone in town had gathered around. The old men in sombreros who had been gossiping by the well came hurrying over. Women holding baskets on their hips put them down and gathered in a knot of colorful cotton skirts, whispering to one another. Some young boys approached shyly, craning their necks to see the dead man's face. One boy dashed up close and reached out a tentative hand to touch the shoulder of the dead man. The dangling arm swung back and forth and the boy skittered away in alarm.

The tall stranger narrowed his blue eyes and looked around. He seemed to be waiting for something. Several sheepherders emerged from the cantina with glasses of tequila in hand and gazed curiously at the new arrival. They were followed by a woman, tall with long, flowing hair that glittered like black fire. Two sharply intelligent eyes flashed beneath dramatically thick brows. A tangle of colorful beads fell across her chest, past the plunging neckline of her cotton blouse, into the deep valley of her cleavage. She wore a shawl embroidered all over with flaming orange, yellow, and scarlet flowers. The fringe swept around her as she lifted her hand to shade her eyes.

"Buenas días," the stranger said, addressing her. He spoke Spanish slowly but intelligibly with a gringo accent. "This is the village of Corazon?"

She looked around at the sheepherders with a grin, then nodded at the gringo.

"Who's in charge here?"

"I am Rita. This is *my* cantina," the woman answered. She winked at the men standing behind her. They raised their glasses and laughed.

"Sí, Sí! Rita's in charge here," one of them called out.

"How about a sheriff?" the tall man said, ignoring them. "Got any judge or lawman here in Corazon?"

That brought another round of laughter from the men standing in front of the cantina. Rita raised her eyebrows disdainfully. She stood with one hand on her hip.

"Sheriff?" she repeated. "In Corazon? Ha!"

The tall man crossed impatiently to one of the wooden portico posts where someone had nailed a fresh handbill. The paper fluttered in the slight breeze. He ripped it off and waved it overhead.

"What about this?" he asked them all. "It says here there's a bounty on this man's head. It says to deliver the corpse to Corazon." He pointed to the dead man draped across the back of the Ovaro. "I killed him. And now I'm entitled to that reward.

Now if you don't have a sheriff, who's going to pay me?"

A short, stocky man stepped out of the group in front of the cantina. He wore rough clothes, all homespun, all black. A rope belt held his trousers but his gaze was steady and proud. The late-afternoon sun gleamed on his balding head as he descended the steps and drew close to the waiting pinto. Grabbing the back of the hair of the dead man, the sheepherder pulled the hanging head upward.

The villagers gasped. The visage was a dark bloody mass. No nose, no eyes, no mouth. He'd been shot in the face. More than once. The stocky man touched the silver Colt in the dead man's holster, then stroked the flank of the pinto. It shifted away from his touch.

"*Sí, Sí.* This is him," the stocky man announced. "I've never seen him, but I've heard the stories. This is his gun and his horse. This is him. This is Skye Fargo. That man they called the Trailsman."

The townspeople muttered to themselves, staring with renewed interest at the body. So this dead man was the famous Trailsman, Skye Fargo, the gringo wanderer who fought a thousand fights, loved a thousand women, found the trails that others could only dream about. And now he was dead.

"That's right," the tall stranger said. "And I had a devil of a time tracking him down." He held up the piece of paper again. "It says here there's sixty silver doubloons for the man who kills Skye Fargo and brings his body into Corazon. Well, I've done it. So, you'd better tell me right now. Where's my reward? Who's going to pay me?"

"What's your name, stranger? You *Americano*?" Rita asked. She played with the fringe on her shawl.

"Sure, *Americano*," the tall man snapped. His eyes were as cold blue as lake water. He pulled off his battered hat and raked his fingers through his dark hair. "My name's Lawton. Rob Lawton." He seemed to be running out of patience. "Now, here's the corpse of the Trailsman. Where's my goddamn money?"

"*Señor* Lawton, there is no need to be angry," Rita said hastily. "The man who will pay you is named Diego Segundo. He lives . . ." she waved her hands toward the Blue Sierras. "He lives up there, in the mountains. Often he comes to my cantina. I'm sure now you are here, he will come soon. News travels very fast here. Diego will hear you have killed this Trailsman. And he will come to pay you."

"All right then," the gringo answered. "That's better. I just want to be sure I'm going to get my money."

"*Sí, sí*," Rita said. "You will get your money. While you are waiting, come inside and have a drink. Diego Segundo will be here soon. I am sure."

The man who called himself Rob Lawton tipped his hat to Rita, then followed her inside. A few minutes later, after getting a look at the dead Trailsman, the townspeople dispersed. The men went back inside for another tequila. The women hoisted their baskets on their hips and disappeared. The old men wandered off to their homes.

Only the pack of small boys remained behind. They gathered around the tall pinto. They had heard many stories about this gringo. Sometimes they had played games pretending to be the mysterious man who was said to be so good he could track a shadow. Now he was dead. And in Corazon. They stood in a silent circle and watched as the blood slowly dripped into the dusty street from the corpse of Skye Fargo, the famous Trailsman.

The cantina was a large whitewashed room filled with rude tables and chairs. Wool blankets striped in green, blue, and orange decorated the walls. *Ristas,* braids of dried red chiles, hung in rows over the bar which was lined with dusty bottles of clear tequila.

The tall stranger had taken a chair in the corner where he sat by himself. His mouth felt full of trail dust, but a couple of tequilas took care of that. Then he ordered some food. Rita brought him a large platter of enchiladas and stuffed peppers. He smiled up at her, appreciating her flashing dark eyes and brows, her tall full-breasted figure and narrow waist. It had been a long ride, he thought.

"Join me for a drink?"

"Gracías, Señor Lawton," she said, "But I am busy." Her eyes traveled across his broad shoulders, lingered on his mouth, searched out the blue eyes beneath the brim of his hat. "Maybe later." It

was said with a smile. "I must take care of my customers."

"Call me Rob," he'd answered with a grin as she whirled away through the crowded room, a glance over her shoulder.

All the time he drank and ate, his eyes silently took in everything about the cantina, about those who came and went. He already knew Corazon was a poor, isolated village, high in the Blue Sierras, deep in the Sierra Madres. To get to the village, he'd had to travel through the treacherous Sangre Pass, the only route in and out of Corazon. All around the little village, the land was poor, the dusty hills mottled with black greasewood, ocotillo, cholla cactus, and squaw bush. There wasn't much water, just one spring that came out of the mountains and trickled across the brown landscape. Only sheep did well in parched country like this.

The men in the cantina were all herders, dressed in black with weather-roughened faces and woven wool serapes thrown about their shoulders. Occasionally, they glanced over at him curiously, but no one disturbed his solitude. After a couple of hours, he knew he would get a feel for the village of Corazon. But there were some things he wanted to know that he couldn't find out just by watching. Like why Diego Segundo had wanted him, yeah, Skye Fargo, dead. How long would he have to wait before Segundo arrived, he wondered.

By midnight, the sheepherders were slowly trickling out the door. The stocky herder who had pronounced the dead man as the Trailsman was passing by his table.

"Buy you a drink?" It was worth a try. Maybe he could get some information out of him. The sheepherder pulled up short and looked him over once.

"Sí, sí, gracías, Señor—"

"Lawton." He gave the name again and reached out his hand, American style. "My name's Rob Lawton. I've come down from Fort Worth, Texas."

"Ramirez," the herder said, awkwardly shaking and pulling up a chair. "Alonzo Ramirez."

He smiled at Alonzo and signaled to Rita to bring tequila and another glass. As she set the bottle in front of him, he noticed her examining him again with flirtatious interest. She disappeared back into the kitchen.

"Beautiful woman," he remarked.

"She's my sister," Alonzo answered, as if warning him off. The herder was staring hard at him now, as if trying to read him. "Many men have tried to kill Skye Fargo," Alonzo Ramirez said at last, "but you are the one who has succeeded. Never did I think our little town of Corazon would be the place where this famous man came to the end of his trail."

"Yeah." He took a swig of tequila, letting it slowly trickle down his throat. "I always heard Fargo was supposed to be a good fellow. Of course, business is business. And I gotta make money just like the next guy. But I was wondering how come there was a bounty on Fargo's head? Those notices I saw posted all around Chihuahua didn't say anything about why he ought to be killed."

"This Trailsman was a man for hire," Alonzo said, shrugging as if that explained everything.

"So?"

"You paid him some money, he found you a trail. Or he tracked down somebody who did not want to be found. Nobody in the town of Corazon wanted Skye Fargo to come here."

"Nobody?"

Alonzo took another swig of the liquor and his face was dark, brooding.

"Somebody in Corazon or around Corazon must have hired him," he persisted, trying to get more information out of the herder. "Otherwise, what was he doing way down here in Mexico?" Alonzo remained silent. From the look on his face, he knew something, but he wasn't talking. "What about this guy who's going to pay me for killing Skye Fargo? The one who put up all those notices? Tell me about Diego Segundo—"

At the name, Alonzo stood suddenly. His eyes flickered like lightning in a dark thundercloud. "This man, I do not even speak his name." Alonzo spat. The sheepherder whirled about and left the cantina hurriedly without another word.

Rita reappeared at the kitchen door and seeing Alonzo's empty place and his abandoned glass of tequila, hurried over, a question in her face.

"I think I offended your brother Alonzo," he explained to her. "I asked him about Diego Segundo."

"Diego and Alonzo," she said thoughtfully, her eyes on the doorway where her brother had disappeared, "they never liked each other. All their lives."

Maybe he could get some information out of her. A woman like Rita Ramirez who ran the town's only cantina would hear a lot of local gossip. She'd know everything that happened in the valley and in the village of Corazon.

"You must have time for a drink now," he said, glancing around the mostly empty cantina, his eyes coming to rest on the jumble of brilliant beads that hung between her breasts. She smiled at his frankness, lowered herself slowly into the chair, and played with the fringe on her shawl as her dark gaze traveled over him.

"*Señor* Lawton. I have never heard this name before."

"No reason you should. I been keeping myself up in Texas mostly."

"But a man like you, so powerful, so talented with the gun. You must be very, very good to kill Skye Fargo," Rita Ramirez said. "Very, very good."

"Actually, I'm very bad." He flashed her a grin.

"I don't think you're so bad, *Señor* Lawton. There is something in your face I like very much." Rita bit her lip and leaned over the table with a rattle of beads. Her breasts were tawny mounds beneath the white cotton of her blouse. "Just how bad are you?"

He took a swig of the tequila, then took her chin in his hand, kissed her suddenly, parted her lips with his tongue, let the hot liquor flow from his mouth into hers. She sputtered in surprise, then drank it in, responding to his searching tongue. Then she pulled away with a laugh and shook her hooped earrings. He poured her a drink.

"I see. You are very bad." She laughed.

"Maybe *you* can tell me something about this Segundo fellow," he said, handing her the glass.

"Maybe," Rita said. Her dark eyes held promises of more than just talk.

From outside the cantina came a clamor of men's voices, a jingle of bridles, the creak of leather saddles, then the heavy tread of boots. Suddenly the figure of a man was towering in the doorway, his eyes sweeping the room. He was close to six feet tall with ringlets of ebony hair, a chiseled face with a slash of angry mouth. His eyes were hard as obsidian. He wore black like the sheepherders, but around his hips were strapped several holsters with carved silver vaquero pistols. A bandelero filled with bullets crossed his chest. Damned impressive.

"That's Diego," Rita said to him under her breath. Diego's eyes found his and in answer, he rose slowly to his feet and touched his fingertips lightly to the butt of his pistol. "You can ask him yourself," she added as she fled to the kitchen.

Diego Segundo's men crowded into the cantina after him. They were armed to the teeth, he noticed, but their pistols were of a kind that had been made about a decade before. Not as dependable as the new American-made models, but just as deadly at close range anyway. The few herders who remained in the cantina silently rose and slipped out the door.

"You must be *Señor* Lawton," Diego Segundo said after a long silence. He didn't speak loudly, yet his voice carried clearly. "You are the one who killed Skye Fargo?"

"I sure am." He kept his voice hard-edged, his fingers on the pistol butt, every nerve in his body alert, ready. "And I'm looking for that reward. You the one who's going to pay me?"

Diego Segundo made his way toward him, their eyes locked. When they were face-to-face, Diego Segundo smiled very slowly, then suddenly reached over and clapped him on the shoulder.

"Bueno, bueno," Diego said, his eyes glittering. "*Señor* Lawton, first I buy you a drink. We will be friends. I want to talk to the man who killed the famous Trailsman."

Diego's men all relaxed and began talking, taking seats all around the room. Rita brought drinks and food. Diego Segundo sat across the table with a big smile on his face, seemingly relaxed, expectantly waiting to hear the story of how Skye Fargo had been killed. But behind his eyes, Diego Segundo seemed watchful as a starving cougar. Diego's piercing gaze would miss nothing. This story would have to be good. Good and convincing.

"I hadn't planned on being down in Mexico," he got around to saying after they exchanged a few preliminaries. "Only I got in some trouble up in Fort Worth." He kept his voice low, as if he didn't want anybody else to hear. "Shot up the sheriff's brother good. So I thought I'd come south for a while. Got as far as Chihuahua and ran out of cash." He paused and took a swallow and felt its long burn down his gullet. Diego was hanging on his every word. "Saw your notices up and thought I could sure use sixty silvers. Somebody said they'd seen a fellow that looked like

Fargo riding south out of Chihuahua on a black-and-white pinto. So I followed him. Was heading up into the Blue Sierras, right toward this village."

"How did you shoot him?" Diego asked.

"Got lucky, really. We'd had a long ride all day and I was following him about a mile behind. He'd never even spotted me. I waited until the middle of the night and just sneaked up on his camp. Campfire was still going so I had enough light to see him sleeping there. I've got a good rifle and I'm a pretty good aim so I didn't have to get real close. Knew I had one shot. If I missed, it was good-bye sixty silvers. But I got him. Put a window in his skull and he never woke up. Then I blew him a few more times to make sure. He's dead all right."

"Bueno, bueno!" Diego Segundo nodded and smiled and clapped him on the shoulder again. Yeah, Diego had bought the story. Didn't seem suspicious in the least. Diego rose and motioned for him to follow. The rest of his men crowded out after them. Outside the cantina, darkness blanketed the town, but there was enough silvery light from the half moon to see by. The Ovaro still stood with the dead man hanging across its back.

"Pull him off," Diego instructed to his men. They did so and in a moment the corpse lay in the dusty street, the bloody mess that had once been a face turned toward the stars.

Diego called to one of his men, who brought a buckskin bag that clinked with coins. Diego handed it over to Lawton. He opened it, counted the money, then drew the pouch shut and pocketed it.

"Well, that makes us even. But I've got one question. Why'd you want him dead?"

"Skye Fargo was a troublemaker," Diego answered, patting the Ovaro's withers appreciatively. The horse shifted uneasily. Just as Diego bent down and started to retrieve the Colt out of the dead man's holster, he stuck out his foot and planted his boot on the dead man's gun before Diego could grasp it. The others standing around gasped and took a threatening step forward.

"The notice said to deliver Skye Fargo dead for sixty silvers," he said to Diego. He put the hard edge in his voice again. "The way I figure it, the gun and the horse and all Fargo's gear belong to me now." Diego straightened and stared him down for a long moment. "You paid for the corpse. I get the rest."

"You're one tough gringo," Diego said. "A horse like this is very valuable. The guns too." Diego touched the Henry rifle in the saddle scabbard longingly. There was something else in his voice now. Respect. Curiosity. An undertone of suspicion. "You're a very valuable man, Señor Lawton. Obviously a sure shot too. Maybe you'd like to ride with us for a while. Make some more silver. You could use money?"

"I sure could."

"And I could use another good gun right now," Diego said.

Yeah, Diego was suspicious now. Wanted to keep an eye on him. But this was better than he'd bargained for. A chance to ride with Diego and his gang, find out about the gang. But first he needed to get a message to the rancher Cassidy Donohue.

"Sure," he said. "But I need a day's rest first. It's been a long ride."

"Of course," Diego said smoothly. "Tomorrow we meet you up there—" He pointed to the dark shapes of the Blue Sierras against the night sky. "Tomorrow morning, you ride to the foothills. We will find you. *Buenos noches.*"

In another moment, Diego and his men mounted and rode out like shadows in the night. The dead man lay still in the middle of the street. Corazon was quiet under the half moon.

He untethered the Ovaro and the big gray and led the horses toward the watering trough for a drink. Then he walked back into the cantina, only to find it deserted. Rita was gone. He swore to himself. Corazon was too small a village to have a hotel. He propped a chair against the wall in front of the cantina and caught a few hours' sleep.

At dawn, the blazing sun ascended fast, a white disc on the bleached sky. It was going to be a scorcher. He stretched his arms overhead. Time to get a move on.

An old man with a shovel over his shoulder was walking up the street and paused to look at the dead man. He rose out of the chair in front of the cantina, thinking it was as good a time as any to get the body buried. The old man spotted him then, starting in surprise as he pulled one of the silver coins from the leather pouch and offered it. Together they lifted the dead man back onto the pinto and led it, along with the gray, down the short dusty street and out beyond the little adobes. The ground was too hard to dig a grave, so they piled a rock cairn over the dead body. When they'd finished, the old man removed his hat and seemed to be saying a prayer. He crossed himself, then walked away with the shovel over his shoulder, toward the village. The sun was higher now and Corazon was starting to stir.

The tall man with the lake blue eyes mounted the Ovaro and sat looking down for a moment at the rock cairn. It wasn't every day a man gets to go to his own funeral.

He had no idea who the dead man had been. Some unlucky bastard, a drifter trying to make a quick buck. All he knew was that the stranger had tried to ambush him. And that in his pocket had been the handbill offering a reward for the death of Skye Fargo.

As Skye Fargo rode away from Corazon on the black-and-white pinto, he knew his life now depended on Diego Segundo continuing to believe that the Trailsman was dead and gone. His name was Rob Lawton now, he told himself. Rob Lawton from Fort Worth, Texas.

He crossed the stream, a trickle of water over brown stones bordered by cottonwood trees not far from town. He had gone three more miles and was cantering northward toward a long line of dry hills when he turned about in the saddle to check on the gray. It was keeping up nicely. His keen eyes swept the land behind him. Against the illumination of the low slant of morning sun, he spotted the subtle telltale smudge of dust rising a mile or so back.

Yeah, Diego Segundo was suspicious of the Texan named Rob Lawton all right. So suspicious, he was having him followed.

2

Skye Fargo's lake blue eyes narrowed as he measured the dust plume rising in the distance against the morning sunlight. Whoever Diego Segundo had sent to trail him was about a mile behind. From the looks of it, two men, maybe even three. He needed to lose them and lose them fast if he was going to swing around to the south of the village of Corazon and find the Donohue Ranch.

He urged the Ovaro forward and it broke into a gallop. The gray was keeping up but didn't have the stamina to go full-out for long. The blue mountains warmed to brown as he approached. The near hills rose and obscured the distant peaks of the Blue Sierras. The horses climbed the trail between the arms of the dusty foothills.

Off to the right he spotted a calm, brimming lake, cool blue and shimmering silver, but he knew it was only a cruel mirage in this scorched land. Sere rocks, dun-colored as the hills, dotted the slopes and rose in towers toward the sky. In the thin shade of the greasewood grew yellow grama grass and a patch of prickly pear cactus grew on a hillside like stubble on a giant's chin.

Then he saw what he'd been looking for, a fold in the hills, an opening that led from the tumbled, sloping land back down to the plain, connecting up with a rift. Far below, he saw the dry arroyo slice the flatland, snaking across it for many miles.

In a moment, he'd brought the two horses up the path to the top of the rocky ridge, then he took a hard right off the trail, descending fast. A rocky chasm suddenly opened up below them. With a sailing arc the Ovaro leapt across the cutbank. The gray followed, caught its back hooves, and scrambled for footing in the tumbled rock, its eyes white with panic. For an instant it looked as though the big horse might slide backward, but it managed to struggle up the bank, with Fargo tugging on its long tether.

The two horses climbed up the scree slope. Fargo glanced back at the trail, which swung into view between the closed-in hills. There wasn't much time. His pursuers would be along any second. The horses had gained the summit and had plunged down the other side, out of sight. He dismounted instantly, tethered the gray to a rock, and left the Ovaro free, then he drew the Colt out of his holster and ran back to the top. He ducked down behind a rock just as the riders appeared below on the trail.

Two of them. Definitely Diego Segundo's men. Even at this distance, he recognized them from the cantina. Their vaquero pistols gleamed in the sun and their chests were crossed with bullet-filled bandoliers. They didn't pause, but galloped hell-bent up the trail. They disappeared from sight into the hills. Fargo returned to the horses and led them down the slope to where the ravine began. The narrow canyon severed the last foothill, then continued as a snaking trench across the plain.

For the next few hours, he rode slowly at the bottom of the narrow canyon, the horses picking their way among the rocks, where once a raging flood of water had carved the land. It was slow-going. The dry and airless box canyon was hot as an oven. But traveling this way, he would remain invisible, not even betraying his presence with rising dust. Diego's two men would fruitlessly comb the hills for him and if they thought to look back toward the village of Corazon, they would see only a deserted plain.

By noon, he'd gone far enough from the hills so that they wouldn't be able to pick him out of the wide landscape. He found a place where the rocks in the wall of the ravine had tumbled down to form a sloping ramp. He dismounted and walked up, leading the horses. He emerged from the canyon to find the broad flatland glittering beneath the broiling sun. A breeze blew, blasting hot, but it felt cool on his sweat-soaked shirt. The horses gleamed with sweat too. The foothills were far in the distance and beyond them the Blue Sierras. There was nothing moving on the plain for miles around. Far in the distance he could see the dark fringe of cottonwoods, the only source of water the small stream. He mounted the Ovaro and led the gray, turning south to skirt a wide circle around the little village of Corazon, heading toward the Donohue ranch.

As Fargo rode south, he wondered what kind of man Cassidy Donohue would turn out to be. It had been a week since this whole thing had started. He'd been sitting in a bar in El Paso when a man came up and introduced himself as a ranch hand at the Donohue ranch down south of Chihuahua. Fargo had never heard of the Flying D Ranch. The ranch hand handed him a letter of folded paper sealed with wax and stamped with the distinctive Flying D brand of the Donohue spread.

Dear Mr. Fargo,
I heard you can help people in trouble. Well, we're having a hard time of it. A bunch of no-good bandits have got control of the one trail in and out of the valley. They've got the village of Corazon and my ranch the Flying D held hostage. Nothing comes in or out without them taking some of it. It's going to ruin everybody. We need your help getting rid of these bandits once and for all. Let my ranch hand know when you could come help us out. I'll give you more details when you get here. I can pay you well. How about $3,000 in gold?
Sincerely,
Cassidy Donohue

He'd read the note and whistled softly at the pay. Three thousand in gold was a nice piece of change. He'd just finished a job and was taking a few days' relaxation in the bordellos and at the saloon gaming tables of El Paso. But the quiet life was getting tedious. It had been a while since he'd been down around the Sierra Madres and he'd never been as far as the Blue Sierras. So after a moment's consideration he had decided to take on the job. He'd sent the ranch hand away with the message to expect him. And two days later, he'd headed south.

The trouble had caught up with him in Chihuahua. First there was a big bruiser who jumped him in the saloon. He'd knocked him out cold. A second man ambushed him when he went to get his Ovaro out of the stable and he left him with a bullet in the leg and a goose egg on his skull. It wasn't until he was nearly to the Blue Sierras that Fargo discovered he was being followed. First it was a feeling, an instinct. Then a flicker of movement on a hillside a few miles behind. He'd paused at the top of a hill, half hidden behind some rocks until his keen eyes had found the tiny figure of a man on horseback on the trail behind him. He had plunged into the hills, circled around the Sangre Pass, taking the hard way up over the steep slopes, hoping to avoid the bandits that Cassidy Donohue had written about. All the while he'd kept an eye out behind him. The man trailing him was good, but not good enough.

Fargo knew the attack would come at night. So he found a secure camp, lit his fire and when it was dark, eased out of the bedroll, leaving rocks in his place. He'd hidden in the sage, waiting half the night until the man crept out of the brush and stood over his blankets, then fired repeatedly and stooped to pull back the blanket to discover the stones. Fargo had shot at him then, intending to wing him so he could get some questions answered. But the man had leapt sideways and the fatal bullet caught him square in the face.

Fargo had searched the pockets of the dead man and found the flyer that offered a reward for his death. That explained why everybody in Chihuahua had been after him. And it was then he came up with the plan to fake his own death.

And now, reflecting on his experience in the town of Corazon, Fargo knew it was Diego Segundo and his gang who were besieging the valley. Obviously Segundo had Sangre Pass under his control and was exacting payment from everybody who passed through. And when Segundo heard Skye Fargo had been hired to help clear the pass, he had put a bounty on him. It had almost worked. He wondered how Segundo had got word that Cassidy Donohue had hired Fargo to come help out. However it was, rooting out Diego Segundo and his gang wasn't going to be easy.

Fargo was brought out of his reverie by the sight of a sign on a tall post in the middle of a patch of alkali. He pulled up and examined it. Burned into a square piece of warped board was the FLYING D brand marking the boundary of the ranch. Not exactly prime grazing. There wasn't much to see but flatland with a bare stubble of dry grass. On the horizon, he spotted a few head of longhorns. He wondered how they kept cattle—even the hardy longhorns—alive here. Far beyond, he saw a dim stain of smoke on the sky. Probably the ranch house. He headed in that direction.

The Flying D Ranch was a sorry affair. The ramshackle buildings of gray warped boards looked as if they'd blow over in a bad wind. A couple of adobes in bad repair seemed to be used as storehouses. A paddock held a half-dozen dispirited horses who didn't seem particularly well cared-for. The place had a desperate look. He dismounted and shouted out a halloo, but there seemed to be nobody around.

A bucket hung over the well, a flat-boarded platform by the paddock. He lowered the pail into the dark hole, listened as it hit with a little splash, then stopped—on rock apparently. He drew up half a bucket, drank a swallow of the warm mineral-tasting water, then gave the rest to the horses. He drew three times more to slake their thirst.

At the tread of boots on the dry gravel, he turned with the bucket in hand to see a young man emerge from behind the barn. He was blond, wore his hair long, his skin the deep, leathery tan of a rancher. He stopped short to see Fargo standing there and his pale eyes, the color of cornflowers, widened. He crouched suddenly and pulled his pistol.

"Get away from that well!" the man shouted. He motioned with the barrel of his gun. "Get away before I plug you."

Fargo dropped the bucket and shrugged and moved slowly not to excite the man.

"Just getting some water."

"*Stealing* some water, you mean," the other man shouted. The sun shone on his golden hair.

"You must be Cassidy Donohue," Fargo said, hoping he was wrong.

"Who's asking?"

"One of your hands delivered this to me," Fargo said, starting to reach in his pocket for the letter.

"Keep your hands away from your gun," the rancher warned, cocking his.

"All right, if that's the way you want it," Fargo snapped. This was getting real tiresome.

"The way I want it is for you to turn around and ride back out of here."

Fargo had had about all he could take from this bastard. Not for the first time, he was having regrets about ever getting mixed up in this.

"Look, Donohue," Fargo said, his voice sharp as a bear claw, "you sent to El Paso to get me to help clean those bandits out of the Blue Sierras. And I had a helluva time getting down here in one piece. Now if this is the kind of reception I'm going to get, I'll just turn right around and go back to Texas. Your call."

The rancher lowered his pistol, but didn't holster it.

"You must be Skye Fargo," he said. But there was no welcome in his voice. Not a shred of it. His pale eyes remained steady and cold.

"Yeah," Fargo said. "Good guess." He waited a moment, expecting the rancher to invite him inside to sit and talk. But instead, the man simply glared at him, then turned around and disappeared again behind the barn.

As far as he was concerned, Fargo decided, the bastard Donohue could fry his own potatoes. He jerked another half bucket of water from the well, let the Ovaro drink it down, then prepared to mount and ride out. To hell with the Flying D Ranch. To hell with the whole goddamn thing. He'd had enough trouble already on this job. Just then he heard footsteps approaching rapidly.

From behind the barn strode a woman dressed in man's clothes. His first impression was of sheer energy, as her very compact figure strode forward. Her waving red hair caught the sun like a bright flame, and her pale skin was freckled. There was something remarkably determined about the way she moved, the way her bright green eyes sought his face, the way the smile lit her face. Behind her came the sullen blond figure of the rancher he'd already met. He was trailing behind the woman like a puppy dog.

"Skye Fargo! Well, and you're getting here at last." She stuck out her hand in welcome. Her words had a subtle Irish lilt. "Welcome to the Flying D. I'm Cassidy Donohue."

He felt the surprise hit him. So, Cassidy was a woman, not a man. The ranch belonged to her.

"Thanks." He held her small hand a moment, drinking in the sight of her. She was a damned fine-looking woman, but not beautiful in the usual way. "I was just about to ride out of here due to the cold shoulder I got from your ranch hand here." He shot a hard look at the blond man he had assumed was Donohue.

"Oh, have you been meeting Cormac O'Neill?" Cassidy said lightly. "He's my foreman. I couldn't run the ranch without him." Cormac continued to stare at Fargo with an icy gaze.

"From the looks of things," Fargo said, gesturing at the dilapidated buildings, "you can't run the ranch *with* him either."

Cormac's face turned a shade darker and he took a threatening step forward and balled up his fists. Fargo grinned back, his muscular body tense, his lightning reflexes alert, ready. Cormac O'Neill deserved a good thrashing. He was a right touchy Irishman with a hair-trigger temper and no manners to boot. And he'd obviously got his nose out of joint about Fargo for some reason. On the other hand, what was the point of taunting him?

"Now, now," Cassidy said, putting a hand on Cormac's arm. At her touch, the blond man backed down and gazed at her as if he were a whipped cur. Fargo saw Cormac's face, and he recognized the look of a man who was stuck on a woman he could never get.

"I just meant it seems like you'd been having a hard time here," Fargo said by way of an apology. Cormac's face didn't soften at the words, but Cassidy seemed to accept them. She smiled and brushed a hand across her forehead as if tired.

"Ranching's the hard life for certain, Mr. Fargo," Cassidy admitted. "But you'll be coming inside out of the hot sun. Cormac, make sure the hands drive those calves in this afternoon," she instructed the foreman. "We can't be having them roaming all over the spread when there's branding to be done."

Cormac moved off sulkily, shooting Fargo a dark look over his shoulder before he disappeared.

"I'm so glad you've come down to help us out, Mr. Fargo," Cassidy said as they moved toward the main ranch house.

"Call me Skye."

She laughed and put her arm through his as if they were old friends. He became suddenly aware of her small womanly frame, how tiny she was as she looked up at him with her steady gaze. She was the kind of woman who didn't have much time or inclination for fancy clothes or fixing her red hair, which was thick and cut short in front, pinned up in a twist above the nape of her neck. And yet there was something attractive about her, a kind of intensity and energy that radiated through her slender form. He imagined what her body looked like beneath her trousers, glanced across the swelling mounds of her breasts under the man's shirt, and saw the small points of her nipples pressed against the cotton fabric. When he looked into her face again, a little smile was on her lips and he knew she'd followed the direction of his gaze, knew what he'd been thinking and she didn't mind a bit.

"Your foreman Cormac O'Neill didn't seem real happy to see me," Fargo commented as they crossed the warped boards of the wooden porch. He held the door open for her.

"Never you be minding Cormac." Cassidy laughed. She paused in the doorway, leaned against the doorjamb, and looked up at him. "I've known Cormac since he was a boy back in County Cork. We grew up together. He used to be working for my father. And now he's come with me all the way to Mexico to help out with the ranch. Cormac's just being the jealous type. When we started having trouble with Diego Segundo, he thought he could handle it all himself. But he can't."

Fargo nodded. And there was more that Cassidy wasn't saying. He could see it with his own two eyes. The jealous Irishman was also in love with Cassidy Donohue, had followed her across the ocean to this dry desert just to be near her. And obviously, she'd never felt anything for Cormac. Fargo followed her inside the shadowy ranch house.

The bare interior wasn't in much better repair than the rest of the ranch. The large whitewashed room with the uneven wooden floor held a rickety table and some chairs. To one side were stacked some wooden crates holding burlap bags of potatoes, flour, and other foodstuffs. In the huge stone fireplace leaned some greasy-looking utensils. Through an open door he glimpsed a sagging iron bed covered by a faded quilt.

"Would you be wanting a drink?" Cassidy asked him. He nodded and she went to a cupboard and pulled out a bottle of amber whiskey and two glasses. They sat down at the table and she poured them each a shot. "To our success," she toasted, raising the glass high.

He downed the burning liquid and saw her do the same without a wince. She was one tough woman. She smiled, seeming to read his thoughts.

"You're wondering how a woman like me came to the Blue Sierras," she said. "My pa was a tenant farmer back in County Cork. Maybe you'd be knowing something of Ireland, with a name like Skye?"

Sure he knew something of Ireland, of the sorry political situation there, but he'd rather she told him. There was a lot about this woman that he didn't understand. He shook his head as if he didn't.

"No? Well, I'll just tell you that the landowners have been sucking the blood out of the rest of us for a couple of centuries. Raising the rents, charging extra taxes. No matter how hard a family works, there's never a way to get ahead. And my pa, he'd been having enough of it. After Ma died, he came into some money. A good bit of money. Enough money to buy passage to America for me and him and also for Cormac."

Cassidy Donohue paused and poured them another drink, her eyes shifting off into the distance. It was interesting she didn't say exactly how her pa had come into that money. There was something in the way she'd spoken that made him suspect it wasn't all on the level, but he let it pass.

"So, when we were coming to America, Pa heard from somebody on board ship that Mexico, in the Blue Sierras, was the place to raise cattle," she said with a sigh. "And so we came here, got this parcel of land, and then Pa died. That was two years ago."

Whoever had told them to ranch cattle in the Blue Sierras had been a fool or a cruel jokester, Fargo thought. He could see very clearly that the land hereabouts was all right for sheep. But not for cattle. Beeves needed too much water and too much grass. Even the tough longhorns that the Texas ranchers were just starting to raise wouldn't thrive in the heat and the dryness in this part of Mexico. There was no use telling Cassidy Donohue all this. If she hadn't figured it out already, it was because she was stubborn. Or maybe she had a sentimental attachment to her pa's dream. If the Flying D just had a clear spring running through it, like the one he'd seen near the town of Corazon, they might do all right. But as it was, with that small well—obviously the ranch was hard up for water, which was why Cormac O'Neill had accused him of stealing it.

"So, what about Diego Segundo?" he asked.

"That bastard—" She took a sip of the whiskey. "He and his men laid hold of Sangre Pass, the one trail wide and gentle enough to get a cattle herd or any supply wagons through to this valley. Whenever they catch anybody coming in or out with goods, they hold them up and exact a toll."

"A toll? They don't take everything?"

"Oh no." Cassidy sounded like she was evading something. "They just take part. They swoop down out of the Blue Sierras on anybody coming along the Sangre Pass. I've heard that now they're also ranging as far as the road beyond the mountains, holding up travelers on the road to Chihuahua."

It was pointless to ask if there were any lawmen in Chihuahua or any Mexican officials who would send a posse down to enforce the law. He knew the answer to that one.

"Times are hard," she said. "You can see we're struggling. Last year, before Segundo took over the mountain pass, I got some stock driven out of the valley and sold up in Chihuahua. With the money, I bought a year's supplies of feed and . . . stuff like that. To get my herd through the next year." She seemed nervous as she spoke. "Now that shipment's coming in next week." He saw a kind of fire ignite in her green eyes. "Diego Segundo must not get his hands on that shipment." Her vehemence was positively sizzling. "He must not touch one crate of my shipment. Or I'll lose the ranch. That's why I've hired you."

He considered what she'd said and how she'd said it. He leaned back in his chair.

"You're hiring one man against a whole gang," he pointed out. "You need a small army."

"All I want you to do is track them. Find Diego's hideout. None of my men has been able to do that and we've been trying. Find out where they rest, where they're vulnerable to attack. As soon as you know that, my ranch hands will help you clean out that nest of hornets."

Cassidy's eyes sought his and she poured them another round. She lifted the glass to her lips, watching him over the rim.

"I see," Fargo said. Yeah he saw all right. He saw that something was not quite right here. Cassidy Donohue was hiding something from him. And that something was the reason her story didn't add up quite right. But like a good poker player he kept his face blank, his expression mild. He sipped the whiskey.

"Three thousand in gold? That's a lot. You could get yourself a damned good hacienda built and triple your cattle herd with that kind of money."

"What good would that do me if I can't move the cattle out of this valley freely?" she asked. "I could have the biggest ranch and the biggest herd in Mexico but Diego Segundo and his men would always have a stranglehold on this valley. Find Segundo's hideout. That's worth three thousand to me."

"Yeah," he answered. It was a good answer, a

likely answer. He filled her glass again, then his own. She could hold her liquor better than any other woman he'd ever seen.

"But enough about me," Cassidy said, her green eyes on him. "Tell me about you. I've heard you're a man of vast . . . experience."

He laughed at that and glanced out the open door. The afternoon sun was slanting across the floor and he became aware that the day was drawing to a close.

"I'm feeling cooped up," he said. "I'll tell you after we go for a ride. I'd like a tour of the ranch." He'd explain about Rob Lawton later.

"All right."

He followed her outside, where she saddled and bridled a blazed roan. They rode off to the east, all the way to the far boundary of the ranch, which was marked by occasional posts. Fargo kept a lookout for the Flying D line-riders. In lieu of a fence, line-riders traveled the circumference of a ranch in shifts, watching for any rustlers or trespassers, driving back cattle that got too close to the borders of the ranch and threatened to wander away. Line-riding was damn hard work, hour after grueling hour of riding, and lots of coordinating work for the foreman to do. But for the big spreads out in the West there was no other way to keep an eye on your holdings, your land, and your herd. Even though he was expecting to come across one or more of the line-riders, he had seen no one. After a few miles, he thought he'd ask.

"Line-riders?" Cassidy repeated. "Well, I never heard of such a thing. I guess we ought to be doing that. I'll have to ask Cormac about the idea."

The lowering sun was a bronze disc on the cloudless sky when they stopped to spell the horses. They dismounted and stood at the edge of a cliff overlooking a wide expanse brushed with white alkali flats and patches of thin sage. Down below, a few dispirited longhorns were grazing, or trying to. One wandered over to a dried-out wallow and nosed at the cracked mud. It lowed, a mournful sound. There wasn't much to eat or drink.

"Well, this is the Flying D. All this land is mine," Cassidy said, gesturing behind them and sweeping her hand southward. "Pa bought this land when we got here and now it's mine. I own every square inch of it out to that butte there and a good ten miles in that direction. It's more land than any of those aristocratic bastards owned back in County Cork. Why I've got more than a thousand acres here."

Useless acres of desert, he wanted to tell her, but he kept his mouth shut. What was the point? Somehow, the condition of the ranch seemed to be her blind spot. As he gazed across the open valley, Fargo could see that as the land sloped gently downward to the east and the north, it grew richer, the grass thicker. In the distance, miles beyond the boundary of her ranch, patches of bunch grass and grama grass grew. While that land was not exactly prime grazing land, it was a helluva lot better than what she had. If her longhorns were grazing out there, they'd be fine. Of course, that was where the villagers grazed their sheep.

"That land seems like better grazing," he said lightly. "Why don't you try to get somebody to sell you some out that way?" Cassidy Donohue turned to look at him with a light blazing in her eyes.

"I tried that already," she snapped, a steely note in her voice. Yeah, she knew what the trouble was with her ranch. She wasn't blind after all. "I offered gold for that land, good gold. But nobody in Corazon wanted to sell."

Fargo turned and took in the sight of the Flying D Ranch one more time. It would have been in good shape if it only had a ready supply of water. Water was the key. He thought of the spring he'd spotted that ran from the mountains past the village of Corazon. The spring must run in this direction someplace. He scanned the land toward the village, found the dark line of river lined with cottonwoods, and followed it across the landscape, where it seemed to peter out, then cease.

"Water's your big problem," he said, thinking out loud. "Where does that spring end up?"

"It's miles away," Cassidy said bitterly. "The spring runs out of the mountains and right by the village. They've got all the water they need. Then the spring sinks into the sands. Just disappears. I never saw a river do that back in Ireland."

"Happens a lot out here in the desert," Fargo said. "It just means the water's gone underground. Have you tried digging some new wells?"

"Dozens of them," Cassidy spat. "We spent the whole first year digging about every quarter mile, trying to find a good supply of water." She pointed across the landscape and he spotted in the distance a mound of earth and realized it was an abandoned attempt to dig a new well. Then he spotted a few more similar mounds. "There's just no water under here. At least none we can get down to." She suddenly whirled about and mounted her horse, then rode off in a fury as if she didn't want to discuss the matter further.

As he followed her, he wondered why Cassidy Donohue didn't just give up on the whole enterprise. It seemed clear to him that her pa had made a bad buy, sunk his money into land that just didn't have enough water on it to support a herd of cattle. Or even sheep. The Flying D Ranch was doomed. So why didn't she just give it up, take whatever money she had left and start over somewhere? Why was she so focused on Diego Segundo? And why was she determined to get this shipment into the valley? Why would a woman as smart as Cassidy Donohue believe that with one more year's supplies she could somehow save her ranch and turn things around? It didn't make sense, but then he'd seen a lot of settlers with that dream shining in their eyes. There were thousands of men and women throughout the West who would risk everything, even when failure was absolutely certain. And he knew it was impossible to talk them out of whatever they had their hearts set on. And Cassidy Donohue clearly had her heart set on the Flying D Ranch and getting that shipment across the mountains.

An hour later, the red sun was touching down on the mountains and they were galloping across a salt flat ringed with tall red rocks. It was almost time to turn back to the ranch. Fargo smelled woodsmoke on the wind, then spotted a smudge of rising smoke, a flicker of campfire. Must be the ranch hands. They turned the horses in that direction, began galloping, and then started racing across the flat white land.

She pulled up alongside him, half rose in her saddle, and spurred her roan on, laughing as the whipping wind tore the hat off her head until it danced behind her, held by the chin strap. The wind loosed the pins holding her red hair at the nape of her neck and it flew like a flag waving in the wind. Fargo held the Ovaro slightly in check so the two horses stayed neck to neck. Cassidy was a fine rider, looking like she'd been born to it. They were almost to the red rocks when Fargo reined in slightly and let her pull ahead. They skidded to a stop, the horses panting and in a lather.

The ranch hands had jumped to their feet when they saw the two horses heading their way.

"Damn you, Fargo," Cassidy said, laughing, her cheeks red, her eyes dancing with excitement from the fast ride. "You held that Ovaro back. You let me win."

Fargo shrugged and she pushed him playfully with her hands, then turned toward the ranch hands and grew serious. Cormac O'Neill stood among them, darting angry looks at him, one hand unconsciously stroking the trigger of the rifle he held. Cassidy began talking to them, asking for details about the day's roundup.

"And, Mr. Fargo here had the idea we ought to have line-riders," Cassidy said. "Mr. Fargo says all the ranchers do that out here in the West." Cormac scowled in his direction. Cassidy caught the expression. "Now, Cormac, why is it we're not having line-riders on the Flying D?"

"I got better ways to keep tabs on the herd," Cormac said.

"Like what?" Fargo asked. "I know a lot of ranchers who'd like to know a better method than line-riding."

"Yes, like what?" Cassidy echoed. "Just what method are you using, Cormac?"

There was a silence and the campfire crackled. Cormac shuffled his feet. One of the ranch hands snickered and Cormac reddened and stalked away without answering. Cassidy ignored the incident and began talking with some of the other hands.

Fargo moved toward the fire. Large hunks of fresh meat sizzled on the campfire spit. Fargo recognized the haunches, tongue, and ribs of a calf. He glanced around and spotted a short distance away the rest of the carcass. He wandered over and saw that the butchered calf was not long dead. It hadn't been skinned and its hide had been hurriedly slashed into strips. The ranch hands had just taken the prime cuts of meat and left the rest. Already a few big black beetles had crawled out from under rocks and were swarming over the remaining meat.

He'd never seen cowhands so wasteful before. Anybody who raised cattle had a lot of respect for the hard work that went into it. Consequently, if the hands were going to eat some beef, they rarely slaughtered a valuable calf, but instead usually picked off one of the old bulls that had already served its usefulness. Out of the tough old bull meat they made some chili or some stew. And cowhands were famous for using every part of a cow, especially the leather of the hide, right down to the horns and organs and hooves and sinews. He felt someone approach. Cormac came to stand beside him.

"Kind of a waste, isn't it?" Fargo toed the dead calf.

"You trying to tell me how to run the Flying D?" Cormac's face was purple with rage. "You son of a bitch coming in here making sweet with Cassidy. I'll teach you, you bastard."

Cormac's hair-trigger temper exploded. Without a warning, he took a step backward, pulled up his rifle, and fired point-blank.

3

Cormac's rifle exploded. Fargo's hand came up instinctively. The boom echoed off the rocks around them. The bullet ricocheted with a whine. Cassidy screamed and the ranch hands all came running to gather around.

Fargo stood holding the barrel of the rifle pointed off to the side. He'd grabbed it and deflected the shot just the instant when Cormac had brought it around. The bullet had missed him by a hair's breadth. Cormac's knuckles were white, his hands shaking with rage as he gripped the barrel, finger still tight on the trigger. The Irishman's face was dark with passionate hate, his blond hair glinted in the blood red sunset.

"What—what happened here?" Cassidy demanded.

Her question hung in the silence as Fargo continued to stare Cormac down, their eyes locked. He'd had about as much as he could take. Fargo wrenched the rifle from Cormac's grip and threw it down on the ground. Cormac's fists came up, his eyes brimming with fury. Without warning, Fargo lashed out, his powerful right driving into the man's belly. Cormac dropped his guard momentarily as the breath left him and Fargo followed with a snapping swift uppercut, left fist to the jaw as Cormac's head jerked around with a crunch. Cassidy shouted for them to stop, but when she saw that it was useless she fell silent. Cormac flailed with his arms ineffectually, staggering backward, his eyes fluttering. Then he dropped to his knees, shaking his head as if to stop the world from turning around.

"Had enough?" Fargo stood over him. One chop across the back of the neck and he'd be out for hours. He hesitated. "Enough?"

Cormac nodded as if drunk. Fargo turned away toward Cassidy, then heard the rustle of sound behind him and half turned as Cormac hit him from behind. He felt the blade bite deep into his side. The bastard had drawn a knife. Cassidy screamed as they hit the ground and rolled over and over, the steel blade whistling through the air, seeking his face, his hands, his throat. He felt it cold and hot, the blood silvery and slick.

"Get them apart!" Cassidy screamed.

Fargo felt the hands of the men around them as they tried to separate them, but Cormac had gone crazy, growling with anger, slashing with the blade. The men drew back in fear. No one could get close. Cormac rolled on top of him, driving the knife downward toward his chest. With a flash he reached up and grasped Cormac's right arm. With the other hand he gripped Cormac's neck, tightening his fingers on the man's windpipe tighter, pouring his strength into his fingers. Cormac's other arm flailed helplessly, the knife trembled, his face turned blue, eyes bulged as the air was cut off. The knife wavered in the air, then dropped out of his fist. Cormac sagged and Fargo threw him off, onto the ground. He stood, retrieved the knife, then dusted himself off. Cormac crawled on all fours in a circle on the ground, shaking his head. Cassidy stalked over him and stood looking down at him.

"I've been having enough of that kind of temper," Cassidy screamed at the half-conscious man. "And I've had enough of your incompetence. From now on, you're just a hired hand. And Willy McGuire will be taking over as foreman. Can you do that, Willy?"

A short wiry-looking fellow with jug ears ducked his head.

"I don't know, Miz Donohue. I just don't know if I'd be up for the job really." He scratched his chest nervously.

Willy McGuire was a wimp and a coward, Fargo thought. Whereas Cormac was a hothead. If he'd been running the ranch, he'd have fired the both of them in a second.

"And don't let me be hearing any more trouble about you, Cormac," Cassidy warned, "or I'll throw you off the ranch for good."

Fargo saw Cormac O'Neill glance up at her with a pitiful look that darkened to pure unadulterated hatred when he turned his gaze toward Fargo. Yeah, Cormac was a sworn enemy now, but there wasn't much he could do about that. Cassidy whirled around and came over to him, took his arm, and pulled him toward their horses.

"Organize some line-riders, Willy McGuire. Like Mr. Fargo suggested," she instructed over her shoulder as they mounted and prepared to ride out. "And if you have the least trouble from Cormac, you come and tell me."

In a few minutes, they left the campfire behind them and were riding under the dusky sky, heading back toward the ranch house. The sun had set and the first stars were beginning to twinkle. A coyote sang in the distance. Fargo realized he was hungry and hadn't eaten all day. And he was tired. He stole a glance at Cassidy as she rode beside him, wondering if she'd offer her bed or if he'd sleep in the open. There was something about her that tugged at him, a kind of pure animal magnetism, a restless energy he admired. She was brash and impassioned, fiery and independent. He liked that in a woman. But there was something else too, something unspoken behind her words that he couldn't quite trust. He decided to ignore that for the present. But he wouldn't forget it.

When they reached the darkened ranch house, Fargo stabled their horses. He gave the Ovaro plenty of oats and water and also checked on the gray that he'd taken from the man who tried to ambush him. He'd leave the extra horse here at the ranch for the next few days, he decided, and then sell it when the job was over. Outside, he heard the sounds of Cassidy dumping some buckets into the watering trough and washing up.

He came out of the barn carrying an oil lamp and found she'd stripped off her shirt and was wearing a man's thin undershirt, cut low. She was splashing water over her face, neck, and arms. In the golden lamplight he could see the wet undershirt clinging to every curve of her small, round breasts, outlining the high mounded shape of them and the tiny points of her hard nipples. She didn't seem in the least embarrassed by his frank gaze.

"Nice," he said.

"You think so?" Cassidy smiled bewitchingly, then slowly lowered the strap of the undershirt, let it fall down her arm. She wiggled her shoulders, until one breast emerged, pale as the white moon with a pink nipple and delicate aureole.

"Very nice."

She looked at him expectantly but he decided to play it another way. He didn't make a move. Instead, he put the lamp down on a crate and sat on the edge of the trough, folded his arms, and watched her. He wondered how far she'd go, the vixen.

She glanced at him flirtatiously, splashed some water onto her bare breast, shivered at the touch of its coolness, and then lowered the strap and exposed the other one. She raised her arms above her head in a lazy stretch and he enjoyed the sight of her. He ached to cup her breasts in his hands, and could feel the pounding between his legs, the hardness swelling, the wanting to be inside her.

"This trough might make a good bathtub," she said, undoing the belt buckle of her trousers. "Too bad there's not room enough for two."

"Want your back washed?"

"Oh, yes." She smiled, slowly unbuttoning the trousers. She stopped to peel off the undershirt, tossing it off over her head. She unpinned her hair and let it down over her shoulders, then slowly slipped the trousers down over her hips. He saw the dark red tangle between her thin legs, the curve of her slender hipbones, her small high buttocks and arching back. She stepped out of the trousers and swung a leg up onto the side of the trough, giving him a fleeting glimpse of her folded darkness, a glistening at the edge. Then she lowered herself down into the few inches of water.

"No soap," she muttered in mock dismay, splashing the water on herself. "No sponge either." She was enjoying his attention as he sat looking down on her lounging in the trough. She lay back and stared up at him. "You're a man with a lot of discipline," she said suddenly. "I wouldn't want to be your enemy."

"That's why you hired me."

"That's right."

She pointed one toe and stretched out her leg upward. Fargo caught the ankle, pulled her wet limb toward him and kissed the inside of her ankle, ran his tongue up the wet smooth satin of her leg and bit it gently. He felt her goosebumps rise.

"Ooooooo, yes."

He let one hand trail down her leg, his fingertips lightly circling her knee and descending along the small tight thigh. His finger entered cool water to find the wiry curls and brushed against the delicate creases between her legs, seeking her warm doorway. She shivered and offered her hand. He pulled her upward and she came to her feet, dripping water, into his arms, her mouth suddenly open to his, his tongue in her, her wet, naked flesh against his broad chest, her small breasts cupped in his palms, the hardness of his wanting pressed against the solid mound of her, her hips moving rhythmically against him. She was small, and it was almost like holding a doll, but all warm and moving.

"Oh, yes, Skye. I wanted you this afternoon, as soon as I saw you. Yes, yes. Just the kind of man I've always wanted. Strong, powerful, afraid of nothing. Yes, yes." She curled up against his chest, her voice husky and breathless.

She unbuttoned his shirt, stroked across the muscular expanse of his chest, and then reached down to stroke him beneath his Levi's. She tore at his belt, desperately unbuttoning his fly until he struggled out of his boots and dropped his pants. His rod stood out thick and rock hard, beating with desire.

Cassidy sat on the side of the trough, open to him, and he stood between her legs, hands around her small hips as he pushed inside her warm, satiny sheath. He could feel her darkness unlock to welcome him in, a key in her lock, sliding in, deeper, turning, grinding into her, pushing his heavy thickness tight in her, cupping one breast. He lightly flicked the fragile nipple as she shuddered and opened more to him, hooking her legs around his waist. He could feel her coming nearer to her climax as she panted, pushing against him, her small hips meeting his every movement, her breath ragged.

"Oh, Skye, yes, there, there. My God, oh, yes."

And he suddenly, quickly, felt the orgasm racking her, her body suddenly tense all over, paralyzed as he drove deeper into her and she cried out, her face twisted, then released as he let himself go, felt the fire begin in his balls, along the root of him, blasting upward like a geyser shooting into her deeper, higher, plunging, her legs open further, hotter, the musk of her filling his head as he came, moving inside her more deeply, driving in, his hot liquid filling her, again, again, until he was finally spent.

She clung to him, sweaty, silent. The night air had turned cool and blew over them. He lifted her down from the side of the trough and they disentangled.

"Best bath I've had in years," Cassidy said with a laugh as they gathered up their clothes. "You do that for all your female clients?" She stopped smiling when she saw his face. He pulled her arm hard, and she was suddenly pressed up against him, her breath quickened in fear.

"Let's get one thing straight," he said. "That had nothing to do with the job at hand."

"Okay, okay," she said, raising one hand and backing off a step. "I understand."

They dressed in silence. He doubted she understood at all, he thought. Women like Cassidy Donohue never did. They were pure trouble. His instincts had been right. She went into the ranch house and he followed, bringing the oil lamp. She pulled out a frying pan and some bacon that looked about a hundred years old. He offered to make supper and she agreed. She poured two glasses of whiskey while he rooted through her supplies and found a canned ham, some potatoes, and onions. He went to the stable and fished some good coffee and dried apples out of his saddlebags, then set to work.

The utensils in the kitchen were none too clean. He'd seen better-equipped and stocked kitchens on a wagon train and he guessed Cassidy just wasn't much interested in good eating. In a short time, he had a meal ready consisting of baked ham with apples and potatoes, along with fried onion rings and fresh coffee.

They sat down to eat and over supper he told her what he hadn't had an opportunity to tell her before, all about his trip out of Chihuahua, about how he'd killed the man who'd tried to ambush him, meeting up with Diego Segundo and pretending to be Rob Lawton. Cassidy listened with her mouth open in disbelief.

"So, as far as everybody in Corazon is concerned, Skye Fargo the Trailsman is dead and buried," he concluded. "You'd better pass that on to your men in case one of them goes into town. And it would be better if they pretended they'd never heard the name Rob Lawton either."

"Got it," Cassidy said.

"Only thing I can't make out is how Diego Segundo got the word that you hired me in the first place."

"I'm sure it wasn't anybody from the ranch." Cassidy shrugged. "None of my men would be acting that stupid. But where does Diego Segundo think you are right now? Do you think he might have followed you to the ranch?"

"I made sure he didn't," Fargo said and told her about losing the men in the hills far to the north. "When I meet up with Diego again, I'll explain that I went off into the desert and camped for a day just to rest up."

Cassidy sat back in her chair and picked up the tin mug of coffee. She shook her head in disbelief as she regarded him.

"You're just amazing," she said. "My ranch hands have been trying for a whole year to get close enough to Diego Segundo to start tracking him and the first day you ride into Corazon, he invites you to join his gang. You'll know where his hideout is in a matter of hours! Maybe even tomorrow!" The lamplight danced in her green eyes. "Then we can sweep in and clean out those bandits once and for all. Just in time for my shipment to come in from the States."

"The States? I thought you said the supplies were coming from Chihuahua."

"Oh, they are," Cassidy said hurriedly. "But there are a few things coming from the States. The whole shipment's coming *through* Chihuahua, you see. Would you be wanting some more coffee? No? Maybe some brandy?"

Fargo took some brandy and they fell silent. His thoughts were distracted, thinking of Diego Segundo and the little town of Corazon, the people he'd met there, the sheepherder Alonzo and Rita, the lovely owner of the cantina.

"What do you know about the people at Corazon?" he asked.

"Those peasants?" Cassidy said. She'd had a lot to drink again. Only this time she was showing it. "Lazy good-for-nothings. Mexicans. Lie around in the sun all day."

"Really?" he said. "I saw a bunch of herders at

the cantina. They looked like the hardworking kind."

"Sheepherders. They're just lazy, lazy, lazy. All Mexicans are lazy. They don't deserve what they've got—" She put her glass down on the table heavily. "And that's what I think of the people of Corazon."

Fargo rose to his feet. He didn't like what he was hearing, didn't feel like spending any more time with Cassidy Donohue. The interior of the ranch house seemed suddenly stuffy, suffocating. He longed to be outside in the clear wind. Yes, he'd sleep under the stars tonight, breathe the free, cold desert air.

"I'll be riding out before dawn," he said. "When I find out where Diego and his gang are nesting, I'll send you a message or come back to the ranch."

Cassidy Donohue seemed unable to take in what he'd said. She stood beside the table, swaying slightly, looking confused. She glanced toward the door of the bedroom and back at him again in an obvious invitation.

"You're leaving? Now? Aren't you . . . aren't you—"

"Good night, Cassidy," he said. He turned and left the ranch house. As he crossed the yard, he heard something crash inside. Sounded like a frying pan thrown across the room. He smiled to himself as he carried his bedroll into the sagebrush. He found a good spot a few hundred yards away from the compound. Close enough that he could hear if anything happened during the night.

As he spread the blanket out on the ground, he

glanced back to see the figure of Cassidy Donohue silhouetted against the golden light as she looked out the ranch house window. He lay down. Overhead, stars crowded the sky. Three shooting stars streaked through the darkness before sleep finally pulled him into forgetful dreaming.

He was up early and left before dawn. The ranch house was dark. Cassidy was probably still asleep. In the early-morning light, the Flying D Ranch looked even more pitiful and he was glad to be getting a move on. He spent all day combing the hills, but there was no sign of Diego Segundo and his men. In the morning, he'd ridden up and down the foothills, raising a big plume of dust behind him, thinking he'd certainly attract their attention and Diego would ride down to meet up with him. But no one came.

Then he decided to try tracking. So he moved slowly, pausing often to examine the faint tracks that led up from the big valley into the surrounding foothills. He found several winding trails and followed each as it grew smaller and fainter and finally disappeared altogether. There were plenty of tracks in these hills—horses' prints, men's boots, even a few wagon wheel ruts here and there. But the tracks were confused as if the hills were trampled over constantly. Trails led every which way.

Just after noon, he decided to head in another direction and rode down to Corazon to where the spring flowed past the village. He followed the water downstream for a couple of miles until it disappeared into the dry sands of the desert. It was an uncanny sight. In one place, the water flowed over the brown stones and green chokecherry lined the banks and a scant hundred yards further on, the water just sank into the loose, sandy streambed. The dry arroyo continued on, but instead of water, the shallow canyon was filled with white braided sand and bare gray trunks of dead trees lined the banks. Once the water had continued across this plain, but that had been a long, long time ago.

He rode upstream again beneath the rustling shade of the cottonwoods. After a while, he stopped, stripped down and bathed in the cool, dappled water. Then he dressed and continued following the stream up into the hills.

The water followed alongside Sangre Pass, the one wagon trail through the Blue Sierras and into the valley. There were lots of ways you could get a horse over the Blue Sierras, but this was the only road that would take a wagon. Diego Segundo and his men had complete control over the Sangre Pass and it was the route that Cassidy's supply wagons would have to take in order to get into the valley. Cassidy's wagons were due in a week and he'd have to find Diego's hideout well before then if he was going to keep the shipment from being ambushed.

As he rose along the Sangre Pass, he saw how many places there were for attackers to hide. Every hundred yards or so he spotted a rock aerie overhanging the trail, an abrupt turn around a blind corner, or a natural stone arch. He kept his eyes open, and his ears alert, expecting any moment to be stopped by some member of Segundo's band. But no one showed up.

By late afternoon, he'd wound his way back to the hills above the village of Corazon. He was thinking of returning to the cantina when he spotted a herd of sheep and a shepherd below on the hillside. He decided to go have a look.

As he drew near, he recognized Alonzo Ramirez, Rita's brother, who had been so offended when he mentioned Diego Segundo's name. Alonzo was leaning his stocky body against a large stone, but he stood up when he saw someone approaching. His wide sombrero hung down across his back. In one hand he carried a stout staff. His sheep, a scattering of gray clouds across the hillside, were being continually harassed by a yellow dog that nipped at their black heels.

Alonzo raised his hand in greeting. Fargo swung down off the Ovaro. The dog came running over bounded around Fargo for a moment barking, then sniffed at him, wagged his tail, and ran back toward the sheep.

"Very beautiful horse," the herder said.

"Thank you," Fargo said automatically, then realized he'd have to begin thinking like and acting like Rob Lawton again. "With a horse like this a man sure could get as famous as that Trailsman fellow. This Ovaro rides as smooth as cream and is strong as an ox. I'm sure glad to have this pinto."

Alonzo nodded, gazing at the horse appreciatively. But he didn't seem to have anything more to say. Fargo yearned to ask him another question about Diego Segundo, but he remembered how Alonzo had stomped out at the mere mention of the *bandido's* name. So, he stayed silent, waiting. In Fargo's experience, men who spent their entire lives, every day, watching sheep graze, were men of few words.

Fargo sat down beside the herder and an hour passed in silence. Alonzo sat and braided bridles out of leather strips. The sheep moved slowly across the hillside and the late-afternoon light washed across the wide valley. Then shadows gathered at the base of the foothills.

It grew cool. Alonzo stood and pulled his wool serape around him and motioned for Fargo to follow with the Ovaro. The herder led the way over the top of the foothill and Fargo saw a small stone hut, almost invisible against the rocky cliff rising behind it. It was well-maintained, sturdy, and neat, with a wooden bench outside the door and a wool blanket covering the doorway, which Alonzo swept aside as they entered. Inside, Alonzo lit a fire in the stone fireplace and motioned for Fargo to sit at the rough wooden table. Then he served a meal of cold tortillas and olives and poured wine from a sheep-stomach flask.

"So, Rita is your sister," Fargo said in an attempt to start up a conversation. Alonzo nodded. It was hard to think of anything to say that wouldn't bring up the name of Diego Segundo.

"How long has she run the cantina?"

"Seven years maybe," Alonzo said. "Long time."

"You never want to help out running the cantina?"

"Me?" Alonzo spit at the ground. "Too many people. Too much talk."

They had another cup of wine and suddenly Alonzo was on his feet. Then Fargo heard it, a faint bleating.

"Los lobos," Alonzo said.

Wolves were the herder's biggest threat. Alonzo grabbed the rifle that hung on the stone wall and they ran outside. The darkness had come on, but they didn't need light to tell where the trouble was. From just beyond the crest of the hill the sheep were calling out and the dog was barking furiously. Then Fargo heard the sound of pounding horses' hooves.

Alonzo swore in Spanish, a long string of curses. Fargo grabbed the Henry out of his saddle scabbard and they sprinted up the hillside.

The riders had just departed by the time they arrived at the spot. Five or six riders by the sound of it. He could hear horses galloping away in the distance, up into the hills. In the last light of dusk, they could see clearly what had happened. Blood was spattered everywhere on the rocks and several sheep had been slaughtered, probably their throats had been slit, since there had been no gunfire. Judging by the tracks of the blood, the sheep had been loaded across the horses and taken away. The dog was circling the spot, barking furiously. Alonzo whistled a signal and the dog dashed off to round up the herd.

"You got rustlers around here?" Fargo asked, trying to sound naive like Rob Lawton would be.

"My enemy," Alonzo said. "He tries to kill me by killing my sheep, little by little." He cursed again.

"Who's your enemy, Alonzo?" There was no answer. "Is it that fellow who paid me for killing the Trailsman? That guy named Diego Segundo? Is he stealing and killing your sheep?"

Alonzo turned to him in a fury.

"Diego!" he spat. "Señor Lawton, you want to find Diego, maybe? Ride with him and his *bandidos?* You do not fool me. I have heard the talk that you will go shoot with your big gun for Diego. Well, you go wait in Rita's cantina. *Sí, sí!* You wait there and Diego will find you. He want to find you, he will find you. Wherever you are."

Alonzo Ramirez whirled about and stomped away in the direction of his stone hut. Fargo mounted the Ovaro and rode slowly down to town, his thoughts whirling. Clearly, Diego Segundo controlled the mountains and also had the run of the foothills, taking sheep from the Corazon herders whenever he wanted. And getting away with it. Why didn't the shepherds get together and overcome Diego and his band? Maybe Rita would shed some light on what was going on.

The large whitewashed cantina was mostly empty this evening. A few sheepmen in their woolen serapes sat at a corner table drinking beer. Candles in thick green glass flickered on each table. Rita appeared in the kitchen doorway and spotted him immediately. Her eyes glittered like dark diamonds beneath the dramatic black brows. She tossed her long ebony hair over one shoulder. Tonight she wore a yellow skirt and white blouse with a deep neckline that showed off the tawny mounds of her large breasts. The hoops of her earrings were threaded with colorful beads and over one shoulder she draped a red shawl embroidered with bright birds. She sauntered toward the table, her eyelids lowered. She did not smile, but looked wary, on guard.

"Remember me? Rob Lawton?" He offered his hand, American style, playing the role of an overfriendly gringo.

"*Sí, sí,*" Rita said. "I remember you, Señor Lawton. You come to drink? Maybe you hope to meet up with Diego again?"

"Both those things would be nice," Fargo said. "And I wouldn't mind some feminine company too, if I could buy you a drink, Miss Rita."

"Sure," Rita said. She disappeared into the kitchen. The minutes passed. A quarter of an hour and he was starting to wonder if she was coming back. Then she reappeared, carrying a tray with six bottles of beer, glasses, and several limes. "Let's go in the back where we can be more comfortable."

She led the way into an enclosed alcove where two comfortably padded benches flanked a carved table. One wall was curtained. She seated herself opposite him, poured the beer and squeezed in the citrus. There was something odd about the room, he thought to himself, but there wasn't a chance to examine it closely.

"To Corazon," he said as they clinked their glasses together. "A very nice town."

"There isn't much to see here, really."

"Well it's pretty from up above. I was looking down on it just this afternoon—I was up in the hills and I had a visit with your brother." Rita looked puzzled.

"Just now? No, now you are lying to me, gringo." Her tone was light and teasing, but her eyes were in earnest. "I know you were not with him."

"The hell I was," he said hotly, trying to sound like he imagined Rob Lawton would. And hell, how did she know he *wasn't* with her brother? "Ask him yourself. I ran across him tending his flock. He fed me a right nice meal and then Diego Segundo and his men swept down and took off a bunch of his sheep."

"Oh," Rita said hurriedly. "I see. You were with *Alonzo, sí*. I apologize. Of course you were." Fargo straightened out his shirt collar as if he were insulted by her disbelieving him. "And my brother Alonzo, he lost some sheep?"

"That's right. Diego and his men took 'em off, I guess. And, after all, what's a few sheep here and there? No offense to your brother of course." He laughed as if he'd made a joke and Rita joined him uncomfortably. There was some hint of suspicion in her dark eyes though. She was watching him very closely as if she didn't believe a word he said. "But hey, I was supposed to meet up with Diego today and he never showed. I spent the whole damn day riding around the hills looking for him. Are you a friend of his? You expecting him here tonight?"

"I think so," Rita said noncommittally. She played with the fringe of her shawl and poured him another beer and sliced another lime. "Maybe he comes later. So, Señor Lawton, where have you been since I saw you last? Maybe you were visiting some friends in this valley?"

The question was put lightly, but Fargo heard the intent. Why would Rita be curious about where he'd been for the last day? Unless she was in cahoots with Diego Segundo. Maybe she'd even heard that he'd been tailed through the hills and that he'd disappeared. In that case, she'd be awfully interested in knowing that he'd spent the day at the Flying D Ranch. And he could just bet that news would go straight back to Diego Segundo.

"Oh, I needed a good rest," he answered. "I'd been riding too hard too long. So I took a ride up into those hills to the northeast, back in that deserted country. I found me a nice cave where I could get some peace and quiet. Spent a day sleeping where it was cool. Found a damn scorpion in my boot when I woke up though."

Rita laughed and her hoop earrings danced. He could see her relax a little. Yeah, the story sounded plausible and she believed it. She poured some more beer and he had a chance to examine the room covertly as she busied herself with the limes. Then he realized what had bothered him about the room. The curtain across one wall seemed to move very slightly with the circulation of the air, as if there were a hollow space behind it, another alcove perhaps. Yes, he could just bet there was somebody sitting or standing behind the curtain listening in. And he could also bet just who it was.

"You are an interesting man, Señor Lawton." He shifted his gaze back to her before she glanced up at him. Rita leaned over the table and crossed her arms. The golden skin of her neck and shoulders glowed in the candlelight. There was a deep shadow in the cleavage between her two swelling breasts. "From Texas, you said—"

And that was his cue. For the next hour he made up story after story about the life of Rob Lawton, whose wife had run off with an actor and who had started wandering around, getting into trouble here and there, never turning into a hardened criminal but always cutting it close, staying one step ahead of the law. And he knew that on the other side of the curtain Diego Segundo was listening with great interest. At the end of his recitation, Rita seemed suitably impressed.

"You are such a modest man to have done so much. And now you will be famous," she said. "Famous for killing the Trailsman."

"Yeah," Fargo said. "I guess I just got lucky there. Never thought I'd pull that one off. I suppose that Trailsman didn't figure on being followed through the Blue Sierras, so he wasn't being real cautious that night. Dropped his guard just a little. Happens to a man sometimes. And if your luck runs out right then, you're a goner."

Fargo heard a deep chuckle from the other side of the curtain. He pretended to jump in alarm, then rose from the bench and drew his Colt.

"What the hell's going on? Who's that?" he shouted, tearing at the fabric of the curtain, then pulling it aside. Just as he suspected, Diego Segundo was sitting in the small alcove, his long ringlets of ebony hair framing the chiseled face. His slash of a mouth was upturned in amusement and he was stroking his mustache. Fargo took a step back as if deeply surprised, his Colt aimed at Diego. He wanted Rita and Diego to think that

Rob Lawton was the unsuspecting sort, a little slow to put two and two together.

"Señor Lawton." Diego rose and bowed.

"What—what the hell?" Fargo feigned surprise and anger. "What the hell're you spying on me for?" He turned to Rita in a fury. "And you bitch, you knew he was there all along? Spying on us?"

Fargo waved the Colt around. Just then he heard a movement behind him and he whirled about, but it was too late. The blow hit him from behind, a glancing impact that made the room whirl.

4

The alcove room whirled around him, the curtains dancing crazily along one side of his view, Rita cried out and pressed herself back against the wall. He fought to keep his balance and consciousness, and managed to become aware of the man who had sneaked up behind him from the side of the alcove entrance. Fargo turned and lashed out at him, striking a powerful arching blow with the Colt in his hand across the man's jaw, an impact that sent the man reeling backward. Then Fargo spun about on his toes and brought his Colt up again as his head cleared and he aimed it straight at Diego Segundo's chest.

"Calm down, Señor," Diego said smoothly. He laughed, delighted. "That was very neatly done. Really. You would be a hard man to get the best of. But now, please put your gun away. I'm sure you don't mean to shoot me."

Fargo pretended that it took a moment for Diego's words to sink in. Meanwhile, Diego's confederate rolled over on the floor and groaned, holding his head.

"I don't like being spied on," Fargo said with Rob Lawton's customary emphasis.

"Of course, Señor Lawton. I'm sure you understand I had to be sure of you. I had—certain questions. But now I am sure you are who you say you are."

"Who else *would* I be?" he said angrily. He jammed his pistol back into his holster and turned as if to leave.

"Wait just a moment, Señor," Diego called out. Fargo turned back as if reluctant. "Now that I am certain of you, I wish to make you an offer."

"Yeah? What kind of offer? And why would I trust you now?"

"I am sorry all this spying was necessary," Diego said. He gestured toward the bench. "Please, sit." Fargo returned and sat down, keeping his expression skeptical. Diego's man got to his feet and stood beside the entrance to the alcove. Rita sat on the arm of the bench, next to Diego. She seemed to know him well. "You see, I had to be sure about you. Because I need your help."

"My help?"

"*Sí*. I need every good gun I can get. I need a man who can track as well as the Trailsman, no, *better* than the Trailsman."

"What for?"

"I'll tell you in due time. Meanwhile, there's first a job we will do together. Just to get to know each other. A wagon train is coming north from Saucillo. We will intercept it and, well, collect some taxes. I will pay you well for your efforts." Diego stood and pulled a silver pocket watch from his shirt pocket. "But we must go now. Right now. Would you like to join us?"

Fargo pretended to hesitate for a moment, looking from Rita to Diego and to the other man. Then he relaxed his expression.

"Sure," he said. "If there's good money in it."

"That I can promise you."

A few of the remaining herders glanced up as they hurried across the cantina and out the front door. Fargo noticed that Diego hugged Rita goodbye and kissed her on the head. He wondered just how close the two of them were. Outside in the starlight, Diego and the other man fetched their horses from a side alley and they mounted.

"That Ovaro suits you very well," Diego said.

"Sure does," Fargo said in Rob Lawton's enthusiastic tone. "I could never have found a horse this fast. Shooting that Trailsman was the luckiest thing ever happened to me."

They rode off into the darkness, heading due north. A mile out of town, Fargo heard hoofbeats and several riders came pounding out of the darkness to join them, merging with them. At intervals, more men joined in until there were fully two-dozen dark riders galloping together in a pack. They rode through the night, climbing through the Blue Sierras, first north, then angling off to the west, following trails and switchbacks known only to Diego and his men.

Just after midnight, a sliver of moon slipped above the horizon and slowly climbed the night sky. The stars turned as the hours passed. On they rode, heading west through the dark hills to intersect the trail that led from Saucillo to the town of Chihuahua.

The land was magnificent with carved rock

towers that seemed like giant's faces in the moonlight and nameless plunging canyons filled with impenetrable shadows. A pack of wolves howled in the distance. A great horned owl hooted long and low. But otherwise the Blue Sierras were barren, deserted, and severe. The rugged crests of the peaks gnawed at the stars. In the moonlight, the ragged teeth appeared to loom miles above, seemingly impassable. And yet Diego Segundo and his men knew the ways through the awesome mountains.

Hour after hour, their horses wound through narrow passes, plummeted down hillsides of sliding talus, trudging along tiny paths that clung to the sides of cliffs where one misstep could plunge horse and rider thousands of feet into an abyss. The *bandidos'* trail-craft was damned impressive.

From time to time, they paused to rest the horses. No one spoke, each man keeping his own counsel. The men used the time to check their weapons and ammunition, cinch their saddles, and examine their horses' hooves. Fargo noticed again that their guns were Mexican-made and many of them a few decades old. Some of them were single shots, the kind of old vaquero pistols used by men two generations back. Nevertheless, even guns like those could be fatal in the right hands. And it was a disciplined troop, Fargo saw, quiet and concentrated. It was also clear that all the men respected Diego Segundo. They responded to his quiet orders with instant obedience.

At dawn, burnished apricot clouds floated above the eastern horizon. The first rays of the sun were just striking the tops of the hills when Diego gave new orders. The men were to wait while he took two others and rode away. Fargo watched as the three of them climbed a series of switchbacks to the top of a tall hill and disappeared onto the top. Fargo wondered what Diego could be doing up there. He looked around, then realized that from the summit, Diego would have a clear view of the road to Chihuahua, which lay just over the next rise. While they were waiting, the men dismounted and stretched out on the ground. Several stood guard while others caught a few minutes of sleep. Fargo found a small patch of bunchgrass and took the Ovaro over to it to graze. The morning sunlight began to crawl down the sides of the hills and fill up the valleys, flooding the landscape with piercing golden light. A half hour later, Diego came riding back.

"The wagon train arrives in exactly two hours," he announced. "There are only four armed guards, two out front and two behind. We will take only the third wagon. Got that?"

The men nodded. Fargo was filled with questions. How did Diego know so much about the wagon train that was on the way? How could he be so certain when it would arrive? It was impossible he could see that far along the trail. The questions must have shown on his face. Diego Segundo caught his expression and grinned, pulling on his mustache.

"You think Diego is one smart *bandido*, eh?" he said to Fargo. "You stick around, Señor Lawton, you will see how smart."

For the next hour, Diego made his men practice

for the ambush. He chose a spot for the attack, where the trail widened and looked benign but where there was plenty of rock cover close by. The men took up positions behind the rocks and then, on Diego's signal, swarmed down to the trail. Certain men were assigned the job of disarming the guards.

"You, Señor Lawton, will hop onto the third wagon and drive it off the trail to over here," Diego ordered. He indicated a place behind some rocks where the rest of the *bandidos* would be waiting with their horses, ready to quickly unload the goods onto their mounts, ready to retreat immediately over the high mountain passes. Meanwhile, others would spook the wagon train's remaining horses and chase them down the road to aid in their getaway. It was as well planned as an army invasion and Diego seemed to be everywhere as he dashed about, giving orders and adjusting the position of his men as they hid in the rocks.

Finally, all was ready and the *bandidos* sat down to wait. Diego gave the signal that it was a half hour until the arrival of the wagon train. Once again, Fargo wondered at how he could be so certain of the timing. He seemed to have a sixth sense. At fifteen minutes before the attack time, the men took up their positions and all checked their guns one more time.

Fargo found himself waiting behind the cover of a large boulder. Diego sat on a rock beside him. Fargo pulled up his Henry rifle and loaded it. He hoped he wouldn't have to shoot anybody. He could always pretend to miss. For a moment, he wondered if he should try to stop the holdup, but what could one man do against a whole gang? And if he shouted out an alarm to the coming wagon train, it would just blow his cover. Diego would know for sure he wasn't really Rob Lawton, wanderer and mercenary. He just hoped the ambush wouldn't turn into a bloodbath.

"That is a beautiful rifle," Diego said admiringly as they sat waiting. "Did this belong to the Trailsman too?"

"Nope," Fargo said without hesitation. "I used this rifle to kill that Trailsman. It's a sure shot."

"Can I see it?" Diego held out his hands and Fargo laid the Henry across his palms. Diego held it up, sighted along the barrel, then opened the chamber and looked inside. "A six-repeat shot," he said. "This is a fine weapon. My men do not have such good guns. But then, nobody in Mexico has such good rifles." He handed the Henry back to Fargo with reluctance.

In another few minutes, Fargo's keen ears caught the sound of approaching wagons, the shouting of men, the creaking of bridles, and the rumble of wagon wheels. The sound grew louder and louder, echoing off the rocks as the wagon train from Saucillo approached. Fargo peered out and saw the approaching mountain wagons covered with canvas tops lumbering along the trail, six heavy loaded wagons pulled by horses and guarded fore and aft by pairs of mounted guards, their rifles at the ready. He wondered what was in the wagons that Diego Segundo wanted so badly.

Just as the wagon train passed by where the men were hiding, strung out along the trail, Diego gave the signal. It was not a gunshot, which would alarm the guards and get them to firing. Instead, he simply stepped out from behind the boulder on foot, taking the guards completely by surprise, as they sat stunned for a moment trying to figure out who Diego was and what his intentions might be. The wagon train came to a creaking and uneasy halt.

By the time the guards and drivers had recovered their wits, the rest of the *bandidos* had swarmed over them. The two guards at the head of the wagon train immediately threw down their weapons and raised their hands above their heads. Fargo grinned to recognize two of Diego's men from the cantina. So, the *bandidos* hired themselves out as guards for the wagon trains, making the robberies all the easier. Seeing the two front guards give up so readily, the two rear guards followed suit, throwing down their guns and raising their hands. One of the drivers fired, but was quickly overcome by one of Diego's men and knocked unconscious.

Fargo went into action as two of the *bandidos* pulled the driver down off the third wagon. He sprinted forward on foot, climbed up onto the driver's box, and seized the reins, slapping them hard. Then he shouted out and drove the horses off to the side, bringing the cumbersome wagon off the trail. It bounced down, tilting sideways, then righted itself as the horses heaved. The wagon rolled around toward the clearing in the rocks, where a dozen men waited to unload. Behind him he could hear the other men cracking whips and starting to drive the other wagon teams into a frenzy.

Fargo brought the wagon to a halt and the *bandidos* jumped into the wagon and began tossing out the goods. He heard a commotion from the direction of the trail—sounds of shouting and a woman's piercing scream—at the same instant that a nearby wailing sound came to his ears. He turned about in his seat and peered back into the wagon behind him. He was startled to see a small child with blond curls sitting on a burlap sack, her face puckered and red. She'd obviously been napping and had just awakened, scared out of her wits. She looked to be a couple of years old. Hell, that's all they needed was to accidentally kidnap a kid.

For an instant, Fargo wondered if maybe that had been Diego's plan, since he'd been so adamant about securing the third wagon. Above the sound of the wagons, the cracking whips, and the horses' pounding hooves, Fargo heard the sound of the woman's scream again and knew from the sound of its desolation that it was the child's mother. To hell with Diego, Fargo decided. He grabbed the child in his arms and whistled to the Ovaro. It came cantering up beside the wagon and he jumped onto it, galloping full out. The little girl struggled like a fish in his grip, wailing in fear. Fargo saw the wagons ahead, being chased and driven by the *bandidos* who were firing their pistols wildly in the air and screaming like banshees. In the last wagon, he spotted a woman trying to throw herself out the back. She was being restrained by a young man who looked absolutely terror-stricken. The *bandidos* saw Fargo and yelled at him, but it was too noisy to understand their words. And to hell with them anyway, he decided.

The Ovaro galloped full out, and as Fargo drew nearer, the woman suddenly spotted him holding her child. She cried out again, her arms outstretched and pleading, until he made it plain he was trying to get the child back to her. The mountain wagon was bounding wildly over the uneven trail, throwing her from side to side as the young man tried to keep her from falling out. As Fargo galloped within yards of the wagon, she leaned out into the cloud of dust, her hands outstretched, her stricken face wet with tears and dust-streaked. Fargo raised the child up and felt the mother's hands grab the child just as the young man yanked her backward and into the safety of the wagon. Fargo pulled up on the reins and the wagon sped on down the trail.

The *bandidos* were giving up on the chase, turning about and galloping hard back to the spot where the wagon was hurriedly being unloaded. For a moment, Fargo wondered if Diego Segundo would punish him, maybe even shoot him for disobeying orders. He considered making a break for it, but there were too many of Diego's men around him to get away safely. And even if he did, then what? So he rode with the others and found that the wagon had been almost completely stripped of its goods and the string of loaded horses were already half up the slope, moving in a slow line, single file up over the mountain. Diego spotted him coming and rode over to meet him.

"Well done," Diego said, clapping him on the

shoulder. "I did not expect that little *niño* to be in that wagon. It would have been complicated. You are a quick thinker, Señor. Very quick thinker."

Diego rode away, finished giving orders, and in another two minutes the wagon's team was unhitched and the last of the horses were heading up the trail. Fargo fell in, bringing up the rear. In an hour, the whole gang would be well hidden in the deep canyons of the Blue Sierras and impossible to track or to find. Yes, they'd got away with it. But what surprised Fargo as he rode the Ovaro up the rocky trail and thought over the ambush was that Diego had managed to rob the wagon train without loss of life. There had been some shooting, but the gang fired straight up in the air to scare the horses. Maybe things in Corazon were not as simple as they had first seemed, Fargo realized. Just what was it that made Diego Segundo tick anyway?

Diego must have felt Fargo's eyes on him. He half turned around in his saddle and caught Fargo's gaze.

"Patience, my friend," he said. "You have many questions. So do I. But they will all find answers. *Sí*, all in good time."

He wasn't sure he liked the sound of that. As they rode through the long hot afternoon, Fargo wondered if Diego Segundo had suspicions he was really the Trailsman? And if so, whether or when Diego would try to kill him again. By the time the sun was setting, they had passed over the high ridge of the Blue Sierras and were descending toward the Corazon Valley, traveling along a narrow rocky path.

Suddenly he noticed that the horses in front of him seemed to be disappearing, walking right into a solid rock wall. As Fargo drew nearer, he saw that the path forked and that there was a very thin passageway through the rock off to one side, just wide enough for a single horse. As the Ovaro neared, it shook its head and Fargo ducked under the low entrance as they passed through the tunnel. They emerged in a small round canyon, all of gray slate, open to the sky above. And Fargo knew he had found his way into Diego Segundo's secret hideout. He dismounted.

The *bandidos* immediately set to work unloading the horses and dividing up the goods, laying them out on the ground. Fargo was curious to see what Diego had been so intent on capturing and was surprised to see it consisted of ordinary supplies, barrels of flour and oats, smoked sides of beef, various tools and implements, and yards and yards of fabric. The shipment was obviously bound for one of the dry-goods stores up in Chihuahua. What the hell would Diego and his gang want with all that?

Fargo walked the circumference of the small canyon, noticing the walls pocked with shallow caves which seemed to be packed with bundles of other goods. From the looks of things, the gang could hold out for a long time under siege if they had to. Several sturdy porticos had been constructed of cottonwood logs and shaded with a layer of spiny ocotillo stalks. Underneath, he saw folded blankets and guessed it was where the men slept at night.

At one end of the canyon was a slope of tumbled rock, the gray stones dark with moisture. A silvery stream slipped out from under the boulders and a clear brook tumbled a short way across the rocky floor of the canyon and ran out between two tall stone pillars. In the gap between them, Fargo glimpsed the valley below. He peered down to see a waterfall right below and then the stream ran down the hill, winding its silvery way toward the town of Corazon and the dry plain far below. In the distance, he could see the spot where the meager stream sank into the hot, dry sand and the fringe of green cottonwoods gave way to the twisted dead trees and the barren desert beyond. Out that direction lay Cassidy Donohue's ranch.

He turned and looked again at the spring water gushing from the rock wall, marveling that this was where all the water came from that provided the poor existence for everybody in the valley below.

"It is an amazing hideout, no?" Diego Segundo was standing right at his elbow.

"Yes," Fargo said. "You have all the water you need. Everything you need."

Diego Segundo looked out beyond him into the valley, suddenly brooding.

"Water, *sí*. But not enough water in this valley. So not enough grassland, not enough sheep. Only that bit of land near the water is any good. Those of us who do not have good land cannot have sheep—" His tone was bitter. Then Diego laughed abruptly, turned about, and swept his arm toward the men scurrying around the small canyon unloading the goods from the packhorses. "But who needs grass and sheep? I do not need them. You see, we have found an easy life here."

"You sure did pick off that shipment right easy," Fargo said, trying to sound like Rob Lawton from Texas. "I guess those two men in the lead were working for you, right?"

"You have good eyes, Señor Lawton. Very good eyes."

"Well, I just keep 'em open. And I thought they gave up awfully fast. But one thing still puzzles me," Fargo continued. "You knew exactly when that wagon train was going to appear in the pass. Down to the minute. Now even if those two men were working for you, that's damn good timing. It's rough country out there and no wagon master can guarantee when a wagon train is going to arrive at a certain spot. Seemed to me like you could almost feel them coming."

Diego Segundo chuckled, pleased at the compliment.

"So, just how'd you do that?" he persisted in Rob Lawton's eager tones.

"That's my secret," Diego said with a chuckle. He took off his hat and combed his fingers through his long black hair, then tapped his forehead. "I have a system. I have a way to see into the distance. It is very impressive, no? Next time I will show you how I do it." His dark eyes traveled over Fargo's face. "But let us talk about you. I have spent many hours thinking about you, Señor Lawton. Many hours, I have wondered how it is that I have never heard tell of a man who is better with the gun than the famous Trailsman. How is it I never heard of you before?"

"I guess I just keep a low profile up in Texas,"

Fargo said with a shrug. "I'm not interested in getting famous, just in staying out of trouble."

"You are a complicated man, Señor Lawton." Diego spoke quietly, as if to himself. "You seem to be many different men with many masks, many talents. But if I found out you were not the man you say you are, I would kill you." Diego drew his finger across his throat slowly, his eyes never leaving Fargo's. "But you are complicated. Yes, there is much here I do not see yet, many masks maybe I do not recognize. But in time, everything will be clear."

Before Fargo could answer, make up something to allay Diego's suspicions, he turned and walked to where his men were sorting through the booty. He seemed to forget entirely all about Fargo, or Rob Lawton. Instead, the tall *bandido* bustled around, issuing orders as his men hurried to obey. Fargo thought over what Diego Segundo had said. Yeah, he was suspicious all right. Diego might even suspect his true identity. But for some reason the *bandido* wasn't going to take action. Not yet anyway. Meanwhile, he would have to be on his guard at all times.

Diego was instructing his men to load six horses with selected goods from the captured shipment. When they had finished, he directed two of his men to their horses. Then he turned to Fargo.

"You, *sí!* Señor Lawton! I wish you to go to Corazon. Take these horses down to the village. When you return, you will get your payment."

"Sure," Fargo agreed, surprised that after Diego's words of suspicion he would be letting him go down to Corazon. He mounted the Ovaro and led the way as the packhorses and the two other men followed him down the trail toward the village of Corazon. Two hours later, as the late-afternoon light was turning to gold, they arrived.

As soon as the villagers saw them approach, a cry went up. Out of the thick wooden doors of the adobe houses, women came, shouting to one another and tying bright scarves on their heads against the sun. The old men gossiping by the town well hurried down the street and a running swarm of children buzzed like excited bees around the horses.

Diego's two men unloaded the bundles and spread them out in the street. The townspeople picked through them, laughing and chattering. A woman opened a canvas bag and pulled out a bag of flour and another of sugar, nodded to herself and directed one of the young boys to carry them away. One of the old men hefted a hammer, balancing it in his hand until, satisfied, he stood and tucked it into his belt. A group of women had found a bundle of velvets of reds, greens, and bright blue. The women were laughing as they unwound the bolts in long strips, cut off pieces and carried them away. Diego's men, who had finished unloading the horses, moved their mounts to the watering trough while the villagers continued to haul away whatever they wanted of the stolen goods. More and more people came until the street resembled a noisy carnival.

Rita Ramirez appeared on the portico of the cantina, shading her eyes and looking out across the crowded scene. Her white blouse was low-cut to expose her ripe breasts and a striped shawl was knotted over her skirt. She laughed when she recognized Fargo.

"So! Rob Lawton! I see you have ridden with Diego Segundo. Now you become a real *bandido!*" she said, coming down the steps.

"I guess so," Fargo replied, touching the brim of his hat. Her ebony hair gleamed in the sunlight, her eyes shone with anticipation as she glanced at the villagers. She lightly darted across the road, her red fringed skirt billowing out around her, giving him a glimpse of lean tawny legs. She joined the women and found a piece of yellow cloth that obviously pleased her. She folded it up, looped it over her arm, and then rejoined him. The two other men were preparing to ride back to the hideout. They called out to him.

"I guess we'd better be getting back," Fargo said to Rita. She laughed and took his arm.

"You tell Diego that Señor Lawton is remaining here for the evening with me. I will send him back later!"

Diego's men shrugged silently and rode out of Corazon. The contraband had been picked through thoroughly by now. All that remained were a few rolls of canvas, a half-dozen bags of flour and cornmeal, and a pile of assorted iron tools. Most of the villagers had wandered away, carrying as much as they could.

"Free supplies. That must make Diego real popular in Corazon," Fargo said, nodding toward the scattered booty lying in the dusty street.

"Maybe," Rita Ramirez said, squeezing his arm. The two dark brows arched high over her eyes as she looked up at him and a smile hovered about her wide mouth. Her expression was unreadable, flirtatious yes, but something else too, a question.

"Diego might get angry if I don't return tonight," Fargo said in his Rob Lawton voice. "Maybe I shouldn't stay here with you."

"Never mind that." She tugged him toward the cantina.

"Still, it's been a long day."

"Well then, you would like a cold beer, no? And a nice warm bath?"

"Hell, you got *baths* on the menu?"

"For you, Señor Lawton, of course."

Rita led him through the cantina and into the steaming kitchen, where an old man was stirring beans in a huge iron pot and a small boy was shucking corn. The old man glanced up as they passed and Rita gave the boy instructions in Spanish to bring buckets of warm water for a bath. She went to a shelf and took down a large bottle of beer and two glasses.

Fargo followed her through some burlap curtains in the back and through a dark narrow hallway. She opened a door and he found himself in a small courtyard to the back of the building, open to the clear blue sky and surrounded by a high adobe wall and shaded by the cantina. A small wooden door, bolted shut, led out the back. The courtyard was paved with flagstone, where a couple of chairs and a table stood. On one adobe wall, a lion's head made of terra-cotta spit water into a small fountain. Painted pots of colorful flowers stood all around and were set in niches in the walls so that the green leaves and blossoms trailed down to the ground.

"Very pretty," he said but his eyes were on her. She noticed and laughed.

They sat at the table and drank the beer while the boy made several trips with buckets of water up a short wooden stairway that ascended to a wooden door. Rita wanted to hear all about his adventure with Diego Segundo and about the ambush.

"He's quite a fellow, Diego is," Fargo said, trying to seem as impressed as a man like Rob Lawton would be. "Why he had all those *bandidos* trained like an army. Didn't even kill anybody either. Just made off with that shipment clean as a whistle. Gotta admire a man like that. Smart. Disciplined. Rare kind of fellow."

"Sí," Rita said, refilling their glasses. "He is rare. But then, so are you, Señor Fargo."

He wasn't sure he'd heard her right at first. Maybe it had been just a slip of the tongue. But as he glanced up, he saw her dark eyes were earnest, probing.

"Huh?" he said, shaking his head.

"There's no use pretending, Señor Skye Fargo."

"I . . . I don't know what you're . . . why I *killed* Skye Fargo," he said in Rob Lawton's emphatic tones. "You saw him yourself the day I rode in here."

"I saw a body dressed in Skye Fargo's clothes on Skye Fargo's horse. And then I saw a man with quiet eyes who watched everything but pretended not to be looking. I saw a man who asked quiet questions and got answers. I saw a man who sat in a corner of my cantina pretending to drink and really trying to find out who it was who wanted him dead. And I see a man who is pretending to be an ordinary man, a Texan named Rob Lawton who just got lucky and killed the famous Trailsman. But you are no ordinary man."

In an instant, he knew there was no use pretending with Rita Ramirez. She'd guessed his identity. And she knew she was right. Even if he tried to continue acting like Rob Lawton, she'd see right through him. He shrugged and took a swallow of beer.

"Well, if somebody put out a reward for your death, what would you have done?" he said in his normal tone of voice.

"Exactly the same thing," she said with a laugh. "You were very clever, Señor Fargo—"

"Skye."

"Skye. You were very clever. Everybody believed you were Rob Lawton. But a woman sees in a different way. You could fool everyone, even Diego. But not me."

She smiled and shook her head, clearly pleased with herself. Her hooped earrings danced above her shoulders. He bent across the table and took her chin in his hand. Her mouth opened to his probing tongue, welcoming him. His hand found the warm softness of her breasts, the overflowing fullness in his palm, his fingers brushing the nipples under the thin cotton fabric. She murmured, a hum like the purr of a lioness. Her sweet lips promised more, promised him everything if he wanted it. He could feel himself harden with wanting, the blood beating in him like a slow drum as he cupped her breast, ran his fingers through her thick hair, felt her shiver beneath his hands.

But how far could he trust Rita Ramirez? Would she disclose his secret? If Diego found out he was really the Trailsman, he'd be a dead man. And how close was she with the dashing *bandido*, anyway?

The boy's footsteps sounded on the steps and she pulled back with a laugh and poured another beer. The boy called out that the bath was ready and then disappeared in the direction of the kitchen.

Rita rose from the table and pulled him by the hand across the courtyard and up the wooden steps to a balcony and a wooden door carved in a pattern of leafy trees. Inside was a light-filled room with a tile floor, whitewashed walls, and a large four-poster bed, a washstand, and a clothes chest. A tall painted wooden screen stood in one corner. In one corner stood a very large copper tub full of water.

"There," she said. "Your bath, Skye." She began to unbutton his shirt, then ran her fingertips lightly over his chest. "Ummmm. So strong."

"But I hate to take baths alone," he protested.

"Really?"

"Really."

He slipped her blouse off one shoulder and leaned over to kiss her coppery shoulder. She began to undo his belt buckle.

5

Rita purred, a deep hum in her throat that sounded like a contented cat.

"Ummmmm, Skye, *sí* . . ." He continued kissing her shoulder and she pulled the blouse further down until her breast emerged, a large ripe melon. The dark brown aureole encircled a prominent nipple. He circled it with his tongue, flicked over it, felt it harden with excitement. Rita shivered and purred again.

"Bath first," she said, stepping away from him and suddenly pulling the blouse over her head. She was lovely to look at, her slender rib cage and large breasts were half hidden in the waves of her long black hair. She stripped off her skirt and pantaloons and he saw her rounded hips, her high buttocks, and the black silken triangle between her legs. She giggled, coiled her hair in one swift gesture on top of her head, stepped into the copper tub, and lowered herself into the water.

Fargo stripped off his shirt and jeans. He was erect, throbbing with desire to be inside her. She was lying back in the tub and glanced over at him, her eyes widening in appreciation. He slowly sank into the warm water, facing her, but even so water rose to his chest and sloshed out of the tub. Rita laughed and splashed him. The warm water felt wonderful.

He lay back and closed his eyes for a moment, then felt her hand underwater, tentative at first, brushing his knee, creeping up his thigh. He smiled but did not open his eyes. He thought how different it was with Rita than it had been with Cassidy, who was all angles and complexity. With Rita, he felt at home, completely comfortable.

Higher, he felt her exploring hand like a small fish in a brook, until she brushed against his cock. Her touch, shy but wanting, was like an electric bolt of lightning that thrilled along his every nerve, as if the center of his desire burst into flame and the fire spread outward along his limbs, up his spine, filling his head. Her hand moved lightly exploring the long shaft of him as the fire spread through his entire body, pounding in his blood. His temples beat with a drum sound as she wrapped her hand around him, moving up and down. He kept his eyes closed but reached out with one hand, finding her breast, cupping his palm against its generous fullness, against the soft wet givingness of her flesh.

Then he felt his other hand tracing the line of her leg, the full thigh, and the coils of her, the springy small folds and the hard knob, like the pit of a ripe fruit. He found it buried in the folds of her and kneaded it gently.

"Ah, ah!" Rita writhed and he heard a small tidal wave of water wash over the side of the tub and splatter on the floor. He opened his eyes to see her head thrown back, her dark eyes heavy-lidded, shining. He slipped a finger gently upward. She smiled at him and nodded.

He pulled away, then rose dripping from the water, feeling the wave of cool air over his wet flesh. He pulled her up with one hand and she came into his arms as he pressed her, wet and naked against him, feeling his hard desire pushing where it wanted to be. She pulled a towel toward them and rubbed his back dry, the coarse texture tingling on his skin. He patted her dry as she stepped, one foot and then another, out of the copper tub. The water droplets clung like diamonds to her narrow ribs, her swelling hips, her heavy breasts, and her short curly dark nap.

They lay down, side by side on the cool cotton sheet of the wide bed and he kissed her, slowly, one breast, then the other, tracing a line with his tongue down her concave belly to the soft mountain and nosing the ticklish fur. She loosed her hair and it suddenly fell around her like an avalanche of night. Her legs came open and he saw the ripe fruit of her and tasted the sweet folds.

Rita groaned, pulled herself around, and reached for him. He felt her exploring lips on him, then her firm tongue, encircling the head, engulfing him in sucking warmth that made the fire flare up again, the flames licking his nerves, his arms, his torso, radiating out from the throbbing that she licked and sucked. The thick rod beat with a pounding in his brain. He inserted his tongue, savoring her musk, longing to be plunging into her. Her hand cupped the heaviness of him gently and he felt the fire begin to gather like the quaking before a volcano.

Suddenly, he reared back and pulled her around.

She laughed with surprise and opened to him. Without pausing, he was pushing inside her, up to the hilt, her glossy sheath tight around him, holding him and contracting, their bodies speaking a language that was beyond words, a complete understanding, a complete knowing. He pushed against her and gently touched her there again. He felt her button contract.

"Oh, oh, oh!" Rita screamed a string of incomprehensible Spanish phrases as she came, bucking under him as he drove into her, harder, growing larger and filling her tight hole until he felt his own paroxysms of release, the fountain of heat driving into her, pushing again and again, unable to stop, his hands cupping her breasts as the heat poured out of him, burning and coming, coming, until finally he slowed, slowed, and then stopped. He lay down beside her, holding her against him.

"Bueno, bueno, bueno," she murmured dreamily. They were nose to nose on the pillow. Her eyes were like liquid pools of still water. "It has been so long since I had a lover. Really, Skye Fargo, you were worth waiting for."

"I can't believe a beautiful woman like you doesn't have a hundred lovers." He tickled one nipple and she giggled. He thought of Diego Segundo. Could he believe her? But he didn't ask the question directly. He never asked women about their lovers. And he expected the same consideration in return. If a woman wanted to tell him, then she would. But he would never ask.

"There are not so many interesting men in Corazon," Rita said with an adorable pout. He kissed her lips until she smiled. "Of course, there was my husband, he is dead two years now."

"You were married?"

Rita stretched her arms above her head and plumped up the pillows. They settled back comfortably.

"*Sí.* He was a very good man, Ernesto. He started this cantina and I came to work for him. Then we married. Very happy, good man. But one day he bought a new horse, a wild horse, and he jumped on it and it threw him off in the street. Crack!" Rita slapped her hands together and tapped her head to indicate he'd broken his skull. "My poor Ernesto. He was dead immediately. And ever since two years, I run the cantina all alone."

"I'm sorry," Fargo said. "That must be hard."

"*Sí.* It is not so easy to make the cantina go. The Corazon valley is poor," Rita said. "You have seen it. The herders have not so much money. But the ones who do not have wives need a place to come and to eat at night. My poor Corazon. There is not enough water for all the land. And so there are not enough sheep for all the men. And with the Blue Sierras, no strangers come to Corazon. Except one day this stranger comes who calls himself Rob Lawton, a mysterious Texan . . ." She poked him in the ribs.

"So, when did you first figure out who I am?"

"The moment I saw you," Rita said. "I thought to myself—that man looks like he would be a fine lover in bed. Yes, he has all the marks of a good lover, strong, tall, eyes that look and see things, a quiet manner. I said to myself this stranger must be a lover like that famous gringo, the Trailsman, is supposed to be. And when you said your name, I knew right away you were lying. A woman can tell these things."

"Not all women," he interrupted. He spent a few minutes kissing her.

"Where was I?" Rita said after a while. "Oh, *sí*. So tonight, I said to myself, let us find out if these stories about the famous Skye Fargo are true? Let us try out this famous Trailsman in my bed."

"Then I guess I'm glad you figured it out," Fargo laughed, kissing her.

"Ummmm," Rita shook her long hair and snuggled up against him. "I am glad I was right."

He watched her as she drifted off into sleep. The ruddy light of the sunset washed across the room and he felt himself sinking into dark waves.

He awoke a while later and saw shadows had gathered in the room and it was dusk. Rita lay in the crook of his arm, her long hair like waves of a dark sea. She stirred against him, then blinked open her eyes.

"Skye, ummmm, *enamorado*." Rita nibbled at his arm, then bit him lightly. He rolled over and seized her, marveling again at the lightness of her waist, her slender legs that kicked at the sheets, the soft mounds of her breasts. She was very ticklish. She struggled in his grasp, giggling, pushing him with her hands. He kissed her and she subsided, running her fingers through his hair. Then she slipped out from under him and rolled to the edge of the bed. She struck a match and lit three thick yellow candles standing in tall iron candlesticks on the floor. The golden light made circles of light on the beamed ceiling. Rita retrieved a comb and sat combing the tangles from her long hair as he admired her large breasts, her willowy curves. She shook out the sleek black tresses, then crawled across the bed like a cat toward him, a bewitching smile on her face.

"Again?" she murmured.

"More?" he laughed. "All right . . ."

"Rita?! Rita!" A man's infuriated voice shouted from down below in the courtyard, then came the sound of boots ascending the wooden stairs.

"It's my brother Alonzo!" Rita whispered. "Quick! He must not catch you here! He gets very jealous." Rita pointed to the tall wooden screen in one corner. "Behind that!"

She pulled the sheets up around her just as Fargo rolled out of the bed and grabbed his clothes and boots. He'd barely made it behind the screen and struggled into his Levi's when the door banged open and Alonzo's heavy footsteps, like the crash of thunder, strode across the floor.

"What?! You don't have to work like the rest of us? There are twenty customers downstairs and you are up here taking a bath and lounging in your bed? What would your dead husband think? He would think you will ruin his cantina!" Alonzo's voice was biting. They spoke rapidly in Spanish. Rita told her brother to turn around so she could get dressed.

"I'm tired, Alonzo. I've been working hard. Besides, it's none of your business how I run my cantina. I don't tell you how to graze your stupid sheep!"

"But you are happy when I sell them to you cheap! So your precious cantina can have my sheep."

"And I pay you and my kitchen cooks for you— But never mind. What is this all about? What are you doing here?"

"You know! Diego is up to his tricks again."

Fargo thought they must be talking about Alonzo's sheep that had been butchered and stolen, but the next words took him by surprise.

"It's not a trick. If Diego wants to make gifts to the people of Corazon, that is his business. Not yours."

"He's trying to make himself popular. That is all." Alonzo's footsteps thundered on the floor as he paced up and down. "And then when he is very popular in the town of Corazon, he can do anything he wants. Anything at all. Diego is getting dangerous."

"It's all your fault anyway that Diego turned to stealing."

"What? You know the law," Alonzo shouted back at her. "And the law was on my side. I didn't owe Diego anything. And you know it."

There was a long uncomfortable silence between the brother and sister. From downstairs in the cantina floated up the sounds of laughter and someone picking a guitar. Fargo, pressed against the wall, held his Colt in hand, listening, hoping to understand what they were talking about. Alonzo responsible for Diego's life of crime? He wondered again exactly what Rita really thought of Diego Segundo. His life depended on the answer to that question. She had promised not to reveal his secret identity. And yet, to listen to her talking to Alonzo, she was loyal to Diego and completely defended the *bandido*'s nefarious activities. Once again, Fargo wondered if Rita and Diego were lovers, in which case her knowledge was even more dangerous.

"So what? You have told me all this before. Why are you here?" Rita said impatiently.

"Because it is happening again. My sheep are being killed."

"How many this time?" Rita sounded worried.

"Six. A few more."

Rita swore softly in Spanish.

"So," Alonzo said, his voice rising again. "You tell Diego from me that if he wants to make himself useful, he will stop them. He will stop them now."

"Tell him yourself!"

"I haven't spoken to Diego for ten years," Alonzo said. Fargo heard him spit on the floor. "You give him that message from me."

Alonzo's heavy tread stomped out of the room and down the stairs. Fargo waited a moment until he heard the hallway door bang shut below, then he came out from behind the screen.

Rita Ramirez was sitting on the edge of the bed, staring off into space. Her cheeks shone with tears, reflecting the golden candlelight. Fargo pulled on his boots and put on his shirt. She did not stir. He sat down on the bed beside her and took her hand. She started and seemed to rouse herself, noticing him. He had so many questions to ask her. If Diego Segundo's men weren't killing

Alonzo's sheep, then who was? Why did the two men hate each other so virulently?

"Are you all right?" He wiped a tear off her cheek.

She nodded wordlessly.

"I don't understand something," he began gently. He needed information. He needed to know what was really going on. "Why did you say Alonzo was responsible for Diego becoming a *bandido*?"

"Diego! Alonzo!" Rita spat. "Two stupid men! Stupid, stupid. I am tired of speaking about them!" She paced the room, her eyes like rain clouds, her arms folded over her chest, her lips held tight. She started to speak again but then someone called from below, the boy's voice this time.

"Señorita Ramirez? Señorita?!"

She hurried to the top of the stairs and spoke to the boy for a moment, then returned.

"I must go. My customers." She came close to him and clung to him for a long moment. "Skye, I hope you will come back. Maybe tomorrow night?"

"Unless Diego has another ambush in mind. I'll come if I can," Fargo said. Her lips were sweetly familiar now, her long lashes a butterfly against his cheek. He took her chin in his hand and stared into her steady gaze. The question was unspoken but she understood it.

"I would never betray you, Skye," Rita said. "I swear this. You can trust me." Somehow he knew she was telling the truth. Rita blew out the candles. Outside, night had fallen and the courtyard was dark. The gurgle of the fountain mixed with the babble of voices and the clatter of dishes from the cantina. The night was clear and the stars were out. Rita slid the bolt of the wooden door in the back of the courtyard.

Fargo pulled her toward him for one last kiss. She clung to him a moment, he ducked through the small opening, and the door was closed. To the back of the cantina was a large empty paddock. He had left the Ovaro tethered in front. He walked around to the side of the building and found himself in a wide alley where several horses had been tied to hitching posts. He heard the approach of horses and a half-dozen riders galloped into the alley and came to a halt. He was surprised to see Cassidy Donohue leading several of her ranch hands. Willy McGuire, the jug-eared man she'd made the new foreman, was there along with Cormac O'Neill. Cassidy swung down from the saddle, not having spotted him in the shadow along the building.

The three of them tied their horses and were moving away toward the front of the cantina when he called out to her. She jumped at the sound of her name and the three of them drew their pistols in a flash. They sure were jumpy, he thought. In the pale starlight, he saw her squinting and he stepped out of the shadow.

"Skye!" She was practically shouting. Fargo shushed her.

"Rob Lawton," he reminded her.

"I'm so glad to see you." She was still talking too loudly. He shushed her again. "I came to town to try to find you and I spotted your pinto out front," Cassidy blurted enthusiastically. She gave him a hug, which surprised him, given the coldness of their last good-bye. "We were going into the cantina to find you."

"What?" Fargo said, disbelieving what he was hearing.

"Why, what's wrong?" Cassidy said.

"Look, you start putting it about that you're looking for Skye Fargo and I'm a dead man. Just remember, Fargo's dead. I'm Rob Lawton. And even as Lawton, it's better if nobody sees us together in Corazon. Or anywhere. I thought I'd made that perfectly clear."

"Oh, yes. Of course. I see," she said diffidently.

Obviously, Cassidy did not take his secret identity very seriously. It went through his mind in a flash that if she'd seen him in the cantina, she would have just come right over and started talking to him. And that would have set tongues wagging in Corazon, with everybody wondering how the Irish rancher just happened to know the Texan who said he'd killed Skye Fargo. It wouldn't take somebody long to put two and two together. He was just lucky he'd run into her in this alley.

"No, you don't see," he said, heat rising in him. "You don't seem to see at all. You can get me killed in a hurry this way. Now is that clear?"

"Yes, it's clear. I am sorry, Skye—I mean, Rob Lawton. Honest." It sounded sincere. Fargo glanced at the two men standing nearby and listening intently. He didn't like the expression on Cormac O'Neill's face. He could read the disgruntled ranch hand like an open book. Sure, Cormac was upset because he was jealous of Cassidy and Fargo.

And he didn't want Fargo anywhere around. He could almost see Cormac planning how to get word of this out so Fargo would get bumped off.

"If word of my identity gets out," Fargo said, "I'm going to blame you, Cormac. I'll get you for it if you talk."

The blond man jumped, then looked guilty.

"What do you mean, Fargo?" Cassidy asked.

"Cormac knows what I mean," he said roughly. "Now what's this about? Why'd you come looking for me?"

"What do you think?" Cassidy said. "I hired you for a job and now I want to know if it's done. I want to know if you found Diego's hideout today?"

Fargo felt rather than heard something. Above the cacophony from inside the cantina, he had discerned the barest swish of sound, like the noise of a light breeze. It was the faint whisper of fabric against adobe, almost soundless. Someone was listening, standing along the side of the cantina close to the front where the building had a few corners around the tall chimney and some outside bread-baking ovens. Whoever was there was overhearing every word. He put his finger to his lips and pointed. Cassidy and Willy nodded. Cormac, looking confused, started to ask a question, but Fargo cut him off.

"Before I tell you about the location of the hideout, I want to know what you're planning to do," Fargo said gruffly to buy some time. He made a signal for Cassidy to start talking after a moment's delay. She comprehended.

Cassidy jumped in with a gruesome description

of taking all the ranch hands up into the Blue Sierras to wipe out the *bandidos* once and for all, putting in every kind of detail she could imagine and speaking in a somewhat unnaturally loud voice. As Fargo silently inched along the wall of the cantina toward the corner, he hoped whoever was listening didn't notice how artificial Cassidy suddenly sounded. And that her voice didn't attract anybody else's attention.

In the darkness, he saw the edge of someone's shape, a dark line, clothing, protruding along the adobe corner. He leapt out, made a grab, and found he was holding Rita Ramirez. She struggled in his grasp and he felt the scream start to rise in her throat. He clapped one hand over her mouth and gripped her tighter. She tried to wrench herself free in a fury, all hellcat. Fargo pulled her back toward the others.

"So, it's the cantina bitch!" Cassidy Donohue said. Rita fought to get away from him.

"Her name's Rita Ramirez," Fargo said to Cassidy coldly. He didn't care for her attitudes toward people at all. Not for the first time, he was regretting ever agreeing to help her out.

They heard the sound of approaching horses coming toward the cantina. He nodded toward the back of the building and they retreated behind the corner to the deserted paddock just as a group of men galloped into the alleyway and dismounted. Willy McGuire kept watch nervously at the corner until they had gone inside.

"It was just some herders from hereabouts," McGuire said, returning to where they stood.

"They d-d-didn't spot us." He sounded scared out of his mind.

"So, this would be a fine kettle of fish," Cassidy said, one hand on her hip as she regarded Rita. "That cantina bitc—I mean, this witch has the biggest mouth in Corazon. And now she knows exactly what we're planning to do to Diego Segundo and his gang."

"Shut up," Fargo snapped at Cassidy. She shot him an angry look but he didn't care. She was only making the situation worse. He spoke low in Rita's ear. "Promise not to scream? If I take my hand away, can we talk?"

Rita Ramirez seemed to consider the question for a while, then she slowly nodded yes and her body went limp in his arms as if she had given up everything. He took away his hand, ready for her to cry out, but she didn't. He continued to hold her just in case.

"So, how much did you overhear?" Cassidy asked.

"I told you to shut up," Fargo said again.

"Let me remind you that I'm the one paying you," Cassidy said. "You follow my orders." Fargo felt Rita stiffen at the words.

"When I'm hired for a job, you do as I say. Otherwise I quit," Fargo said, his voice like iron. "Right here and right now. Your choice."

Cassidy set her chin and tightened her mouth, then nodded. Her eyes glowed like two green flames in the starlight. She was hopping mad. Cormac, standing to one side, was smirking.

"You are playing a dangerous game, Skye Fargo,"

Rita said in a low voice. He felt her breath catch, as if she were holding back a sob.

"You swore you wouldn't tell my identity," he said. "After what you overheard, is that still true?"

Rita sobbed silently in his arms as if she were being torn in pieces by some terrible sorrow, as if the question was posing a painful dilemma to her. But finally she nodded yes.

"*Sí*, I swear."

"Ridiculous!" Cassidy cut in. "You can't be trusting these Mexican peasants. They lie like a Welshman. Soon as we ride out of here, she'll go straight to her pal Diego. Before you know it, she'll tell him everything. And that will spoil our whole plan and the shipment will be lost. My whole ranch will be lost. I say we kill her."

"*What?*"

"Kill her right here." Cassidy's voice was as cold as a frozen lake. "Nobody would know for hours and by then, we'll have wiped out Segundo's gang."

"*You're* the bitch," Fargo said. Cassidy gasped. He let loose of Rita and advanced on Cassidy. Cormac stepped up, his pale hair gleaming in the starlight. Without warning, Cormac brought his fist up in a whistling right, but Fargo was too fast. He blocked it and with his powerful left delivered a lightning left in Cormac's midsection. The man gasped for breath and Fargo rammed him against the adobe wall, lifting him up off his feet. There was a thud as Cormac's head hit hard, his knees gave way, and he slid slowly down the wall.

"We don't have time to fight each other," Fargo said.

"That's right," Cassidy agreed. Her voice was smooth, controlled. "I apologize, Skye. If I'd known you had a soft spot for Mexicans I wouldn't have suggested killing the girl. But she's tight with Diego Segundo. Everybody knows that. And I don't trust her. I'll do anything to save my ranch, everything I've worked for."

"Even kill innocent people?" Fargo shot back at her.

"Of course not," Cassidy said hurriedly.

"Well, I don't trust *him*," Cormac said, getting to his feet. He braced himself against the wall as he swayed back and forth. As Cormac rubbed his jaw, he glared at Fargo. "I say he's the one's going to double-cross us."

"That's enough. Get back to the ranch, Cormac," Cassidy said. "Now. And tell the rest of the men I want them on guard. Just in case something goes wrong, I want the ranch ready for an attack. Now get."

The blond rancher stomped off, mounted, and rode away.

Despite her conciliatory words about Rita, Fargo was fed up with Cassidy's intolerant attitude as well as the belligerent Cormac and the hopelessly doomed Flying D Ranch. Things were much more complicated than they had first appeared. He just wanted to ride out of Corazon and forget the whole damn mess. But he realized if he left now, Rita's life would be in danger. Cassidy didn't trust her silence, didn't trust that she wouldn't tell Diego Segundo the ranch hands were going to wipe out the gang.

And there was something else going on here. Diego Segundo wasn't exactly the outlaw he'd expected. Segundo had managed the ambush without killing anybody. Not that it made stealing all right of course. But then he distributed a lot of the booty free to the villagers of Corazon.

Then there was Cassidy. He was sure she wasn't telling him the whole story. Nobody was. Nothing added up in this crazy little town. As he considered his options, he looked at Rita. She stood defiant, her head held high as if challenging him. Deep in his heart he knew he could trust her. She had sworn she wouldn't betray him and he believed her. But could he take the risk? One thing was certain. The longer they lingered in Corazon out in the open behind the cantina, the more likely it was that somebody would discover them there, somebody like Diego's men. He needed to get them all someplace safe and quiet where he could question Cassidy and Rita and get to the very bottom of the whole thing. And then he could decide what to do.

"We're going back to the Flying D," he said. "And you're coming with us, Rita. I need you there." Rita shot a frightened look at him. "Trust me. You'll be safe," he assured her.

Willy McGuire watched over Rita while Fargo fetched the Ovaro from in front of the cantina. As the others mounted, he lifted Rita onto the pinto and mounted behind her, encircling her with his strong arms. Rita lay back against his chest.

"Comfortable?" Cassidy asked sarcastically.

Rather than leave the town by the main road, Fargo led them at a slow walk back along the side of the paddock through several dark alleys to the edge of town, where the small adobes gave way to the open starlit land. He was alert to any sound or movement. The little town was quiet and they saw no one. Fargo hoped no one had seen or recognized them.

At the edge of town, the Ovaro started forward in an easy canter across the wide land. Fargo decided they would head down to the little stream and ride under cover of the trees until the stream ended along with the trees. They'd be a couple of miles from the town of Corazon and they could cross the miles and miles across the dark desert land to the Flying D Ranch.

Cassidy Donohue spurred her horse forward into a gallop as if eager to leave Fargo in her dust. Willy McGuire followed close behind. Fargo let them get ahead and felt the Ovaro eager beneath him, straining to ride full out. He held the powerful pinto in check and fell behind to bring up the rear.

"Are you really planning to kill Diego?" Rita said to him. "I can't believe you would do such a thing."

"I don't know," Fargo said honestly. "I've got a lot of questions. We'll talk about it when we get to the ranch." He cantered down the sloping land. Ahead lay the dark line of cottonwoods, the leaves sparkling like silver in the faint light. Cassidy and Willy McGuire disappeared into the dark shadows of the trees.

Suddenly, he knew they were not alone. An instinct honed from his long years in the wild told him that he was about to ride into danger, but this time the instinct came too late. The trees were coming on fast. In a split second, the pop of gunfire erupted from the shadowy cottonwoods where Cassidy and McGuire had gone in. He could see nothing in the blackness by the stream. Rita was pressed hard against him, afraid. The Colt was in his hand. It was too late to turn the Ovaro aside as they plunged into the shadows between the trunks.

A dozen riders suddenly materialized on either side of him, riding up to surround him. It was hopeless to resist. Fargo holstered his Colt.

"Put your hands in the air, Señor Fargo. *Sí*, Señor Skye Fargo, the Trailsman."

It was the voice of Diego Segundo.

6

Diego Segundo's voice called out again over the pounding of horses' hooves and the jangle of spurs and bridles.

"Put your hands up in the air, Señor Skye Fargo. And don't touch your pistol or I'll shoot."

"Don't shoot, don't shoot, Mr. Segundo! I surrender!" It was Willy McGuire and he sounded scared out of his wits.

Fargo's eyes adjusted to the darkness beneath the cottonwoods and he saw that Diego Segundo was on an Appaloosa. Most of his riders were there. All of them had their pistols drawn. There was no escape. Not at the moment, anyway.

"Diego!" Rita called out. "Diego, it's me, Rita!"

"Get down," Diego ordered them all in a cold voice, seeming unsurprised that Rita was with them. In the shimmering shadows of the night, he could just make out their faces as everyone dismounted. The gang surrounded the four of them, pressing them into a circle. "Hand over your weapons," Diego ordered. Fargo hesitated, but realized if he started shooting he would just get them all killed. He reluctantly threw down the Colt, Cassidy her old pistol, and McGuire his hunting rifle. One of Diego's men retrieved the Colt and held it in his hand admiringly. Once again, Fargo noticed the outdated rifles and pistols that Diego and his men were using. Diego walked back and forth in front of the four of them. He stopped in front of Willy McGuire, pulled his silver vaquero pistol, and held it at eye level in front of the man's face.

"What do you have to say for yourself? Talk."

"Sure, sure." McGuire sounded completely terrified. "He's the T-T-Trailsman, all right," McGuire babbled, his voice quivering.

"Shut up," Cassidy hissed. Diego cocked his pistol. McGuire stared down the barrel. Even in the darkness, Fargo could see the ranch hand quaking with fear.

"Oh, *really*?" Diego said. "He's the Trailsman? He doesn't look dead to me. Tell me something I *don't* know. Like what is your boss lady, Cassidy Donohue, planning to do?"

"Shut up, McGuire," Cassidy warned. "Don't tell him anything." But it was no good. Willy McGuire's wide eyes were fixed on the huge black barrel in front of his face as if it were a swaying cobra. And he was a complete coward, through and through. The threat was enough to make him tell everything.

"Well, F-F-Fargo found out where your h-h-hideout is. And he was going to t-t-take us there, us ranch hands, so we could—" McGuire faltered and stopped. His knees were shaking so badly, he could scarcely stand up. He started to sink down and one of the *bandidos* stepped up behind and held him upright by the collar.

"I see," Diego said quietly. He started to holster the pistol, then suddenly swung it in an arc and smashed Willy McGuire across the jaw. The man screamed and went down to the ground. "I hate weakness, disloyalty," Diego remarked under his breath, as if talking to himself. Willy McGuire groaned and lay in a crumpled heap on the ground.

"Don't kill us, please," Cassidy started in. She was about to crack too.

"So, how did you find us, Diego?" Fargo spoke up to distract the *bandido*'s attention and give Cassidy a moment to recover her wits.

"One of my men was following you, Señor," Diego said. "When you went to town with the supplies. I wanted to know what trouble you might get into. Little did I know—"

Diego suddenly grabbed Rita's arm and pulled her toward him roughly. Fargo took a step forward protectively and Diego, seeing that, barked a strange laugh.

"Rita, why are you riding with this gringo?" Diego asked. "Don't you know he is really the Trailsman? He is a dangerous man."

Rita stared defiantly into Diego's face. Any other woman would have talked, would have told Diego everything to save her own skin. But Rita Ramirez remained silent.

"Let her go," Fargo said. "She doesn't know anything. It's my fault. I was kidnapping her from Corazon."

Diego Segundo laughed the strange laugh again and pushed Rita away from him toward his men. He came up close to stare at Fargo.

"I respect a man who can tell a good lie when it's needed." Diego's voice was quiet as the rustle of a rattlesnake.

"So, when did you figure out I'm the Trailsman?" There was no use pretending anymore. That game was over.

"I had a feeling about you from the very beginning," Diego said with a slow smile. "But I was not sure. So during the ambush, I was watching you. I saw a man who makes quick decisions, who rides well, thinks clearly, uses his head. I knew then that you were not this ordinary Texas man that you claimed to be. But I still did not know what your game might be. There was something about you that made me think maybe my information was wrong."

"What information was that?"

"I received word that this Irish lady had hired the Trailsman to help her make trouble for Corazon. So I put up some notices just in case you came this way. Then when I met you, I thought if you really were the Trailsman—well, you seemed like you were a different kind of a man and that perhaps the Trailsman would see . . ."

"Would see *what*?"

Diego stamped his foot and swore a string of Spanish curses.

"Never mind. It was a stupid idea. Gringos stick together. And now I know for sure you are working for *her* and what you were planning to do."

The *bandido* had hardly glanced in Cassidy's direction and had barely spoken to her either. Yet Fargo could feel in the silence that lay between them a bitter enmity. Diego suddenly turned and spat at her feet. He walked up and stood directly in front of her and she returned his gaze defiantly.

"You think you can own everything. But you can't," Diego said to Cassidy. Then he suddenly whirled around, turning his back on her. "Let's go," Diego said. Without another order, the men pressed forward.

Fargo felt himself being seized from behind. For a moment, he tensed, ready to fight, and then realized it was pointless. They were tying up Cassidy and McGuire too. Fargo concentrated on holding his wrists apart and rotating them slightly as his hands were bound together behind his back. When the knots were tied, he could feel the ropes had some slack in them. Yeah, he could work out of them.

They were trying to get Willy McGuire up onto a horse. Suddenly, there was a flurry of movement and McGuire barreled forward into one of the *bandidos,* trying to knock him to the ground and make an escape. Instinctively, the *bandido* drew and fired. The explosion shook the air and the bullet struck McGuire right in the chest. He dropped to the ground, dead in one instant.

"Stupido," Diego said, kicking McGuire's body. "Don't try anything like that," he said to Cassidy and Fargo. She nodded. Fargo could see that despite her usual bluster, she was scared now, not knowing what would happen. Fargo could guess the first part. They were being taken up to the hideout. If Diego just wanted to kill them, he would go ahead and do it here and now, wouldn't he? Maybe there was something else he wanted,

but Fargo couldn't imagine what it was. He was sure it had to do with the heavy hatred that he felt between Diego and Cassidy Donohue.

Diego called for the Ovaro to be brought. He patted the pinto on the nose and tried to mount. It shied away, not trusting any rider but Fargo. Diego swore and tried again. He managed to slip into the saddle, but the pinto reared up then bucked. The *bandidos* moved away and Diego jumped off the horse before he could be thrown.

"Very loyal horse," he said to Fargo with an appreciative laugh. "Put the two of them on some other one. I will lead this beautiful one behind my own."

Fargo and Cassidy were put together onto a heavy bay, with Cassidy sitting in front of him. He could feel her trembling. The horse they were riding looked powerful, a thick-legged draft horse which looked like it could carry a lot of weight. But it wasn't fast. That was a good move, Fargo thought to himself. Put the prisoners on a draft horse just in case they had any ideas of escape. Exactly what he would do if he were in Diego's shoes. Once again, he found himself with a grudging admiration for the *bandido*. The gang formed up into a double line with several extra men riding alongside the two prisoners. Diego was in the lead, with the Ovaro tethered behind him.

"Get back to town," Diego said in Spanish to Rita. He instructed one of his men to bring her a horse.

"No!" she said. "I'm going with you. I don't want you to hurt Fargo! He's a good man! Don't shoot him, please." She was pleading with Diego now, holding on to him as he prepared to ride out. "Please don't hurt him."

"Do as I say," Diego said, pushing her away. Rita burst into tears as she got onto the horse. She glanced over her shoulder at Fargo and then rode away reluctantly. Diego sent one of his men with her to make sure she got back to the cantina and stayed there.

They started off, the line of horses moving slowly beneath the cottonwoods. Diego sent several men as outriders in front and to the rear to keep an eye out for anyone in the vicinity. Diego was cautious and practiced, Fargo thought. A man who knew how to do things right. Cassidy was sitting on the saddle in front of him, her compact frame pressed up against his broad chest.

"He's going to kill us," Cassidy whispered over her shoulder.

"I'll get us out," Fargo responded into her ear. "Just be ready to do as I say."

"Silence!" one of Diego's men called out to them.

As they rode, Fargo worked on the ropes that bound his hands, twisting and pulling but trying not to make too much motion to attract attention. After a few miles, he found he could slip one hand out. They were riding in the darkness under the trees where the land trail began to climb into the foothills.

"Don't move," Fargo whispered in Cassidy's ear. "In a minute or two, I'm going to put a knife in your hands. Get ready to hold on to it."

She nodded. He would need a lot of luck now. If anyone happened to be staring at him from behind, the jig would be up. But maybe, just maybe, their attention would be diverted. They rode on another quarter mile to where the foothills began as he waited for an opportunity. Here the path narrowed and the gang was forced to ride strung out, single file. This was their best chance. In another mile or two the land would become rocky and steep, the narrow trail clinging to the sides of cliffs. It would be impossible to leave the trail without plunging off into an abyss. They would have to make a move before they reached the higher peaks. And yet the heavy bay they rode would never be able to outrun Diego's gang.

Just then, one of the men shouted. Something up ahead, just off the trail. The horses came to a halt. Diego's men were immediately alert. They slid their pistols out of their holsters and craned their necks to see. This was it. Fargo slid one hand out of the ropes, leaving the other behind his back. He pulled up his right pant leg and slipped the Arkansas toothpick from the ankle scabbard, reached around in front of him and put it into Cassidy's bound hands, then returned his right hand to hold it behind his back, wrapped in the rope as if bound tight. The whole thing had taken a scant few seconds.

He waited a moment, expecting the man riding behind him to notice his movement and raise an alarm. But there was a long silence as all the gang concentrated on what was up ahead.

"Saw through the ropes," he instructed Cassidy in the barest whisper. "Nod when you're finished."

Several of the *bandidos* up ahead began laughing

and Fargo saw a lamb emerge from the tall scraggly thornbushes that lined the trail along this stretch. The lamb tottered on wobbly legs and bleated forlornly. In another moment, a wooly ewe came scrambling up the hillside, ducked under the bushes, and nosed the lamb away from the trail. Diego's men relaxed again, holstered their pistols, and the procession proceeded. Fargo realized they were near the area where Alonzo kept his flock.

Cassidy had been working the knife back and forth on the rope. Just then Diego turned about in his saddle and stared back at them as if he could read their minds. Fargo felt Cassidy stiffen, freeze. Fargo swore silently, hoping the knife blade would not glint in the dim starlight. After a moment, Diego turned about and Cassidy started in again. It was slow going, holding the knife awkwardly between her bound hands while trying to move it back and forth against the tight ropes. Nevertheless, the blade was exceedingly sharp and he looked over her shoulder to see that the rope was beginning to fray.

They had gone another half mile when the rope gave way. Fargo felt the jolt as Cassidy pulled her hands apart. In surprise, she almost dropped the knife, but then fumbled and barely managed to grab the handle just before it dropped to the ground. The sudden movement attracted the attention of the *bandido* riding just behind them. He grunted in surprise and spurred his horse to get a closer look at them. It was now or never, Fargo realized.

He suddenly brought his arms around and

pulled the bay's nose to a hard right with brutal force. Surprised, the heavy horse plunged off the trail into the thornbushes. Several of the gang shouted an alarm and shots rang out. Fargo ducked low over Cassidy.

"I want them alive!" Diego shouted. "Alive!"

The bay stumbled down off the trail, carried forward by the momentum of its own weight. The horse fought through the bushes, shrieking in shock and pain as it was pierced by the sharp thorns. Fargo felt the sting of thorns in his leg and Cassidy cried out. The horse leapt, trying to clear the painful barbs, then took off in a gallop, hell-bent across the rocky hillside. Fargo hadn't counted on the thorns but realized they'd been damned lucky. The pain was about the only thing that would get the lethargic horse going. And it was going to keep galloping with dozens of thorns driven deep in its tender skin.

As they neared the top of the hill, Fargo turned about to look behind them. Diego's men found it impossible to persuade their horses to follow through the thorns. The horses were rearing in protest. But he could also see that several others were galloping up the trail and would circle around the thorny patch. They reached the summit, galloped over, and lost sight of the gang.

Below on the starlit slope was a blanket of sheep, packed close together, some sleeping, some milling about on their feet. It would be only a matter of moments before Diego's men caught up with their slow-moving bay, despite the thorns.

"Jump!" he warned Cassidy a split second before he put his arms around her and pitched sideways, plunging through the air and hitting a patch of bunchgrass. The bay galloped on blindly, whinnying in pain, all the faster for not carrying the two of them. They rolled over once and then Fargo jumped to his feet, pulling Cassidy along with him.

"Move slowly," he said. "And follow me."

She groaned with the pain of the thorns in her legs and he would have liked to stop and pull out the few that were burning him as well, but they had to keep moving. They made their way down the hillside to where the sheep were resting. Several of the sheep got to their feet nervously, but most continued dozing.

Alonzo's yellow dog came up barking and Fargo put out his hand. The dog sniffed it, recognized him, wagged its tail, and moved off down the slope to bring back a few wanderers. They moved further into the flock. There was not a moment to lose. Fargo suddenly dropped to his knees, then lay down on the ground, pulling Cassidy along with him. He guessed they couldn't be spotted among the nubby backs of the sheep. Especially in the darkness. They crawled forward to where the sheep were thickest.

"Damn stinky critters," Fargo said. Cassidy didn't respond and he could tell from the stiffness of her small frame that she was scared through and through. In another instant, he heard the pounding of hooves as several of Diego's men galloped over the summit and plunged down the hillside, following the bay. Fargo raised his head and looked out. Several more riders appeared heading in the same direction, then several more. Finally, he saw on the summit of the hill one man sitting on an Appaloosa. He was leading the black-and-white pinto. Fargo recognized the figure of Diego Segundo, who sat staring down at the flock of sheep. Clearly he was the only one who had suspected where Fargo had really gone.

Fargo gave a low, long whistle, then a short one. The response was immediate. On the summit, the Ovaro reared up on its hind legs and neighed in response. The Appaloosa shied away and the tether between the two horses was stretched tight. The Ovaro reared again and came down hard, right beside the other horse, which began to panic. It sidestepped as the Ovaro shouldered it and bit its flanks. Diego Segundo swatted at the Ovaro with his quirt but suddenly it was too late. The Appaloosa reared up along with the Ovaro. Diego Segundo tried desperately to keep his seat, but fell to the earth.

Fargo stood and whistled again. The Ovaro pushed the other horse down the hill, nipping at its withers. Fargo could hear Diego Segundo shouting in a fury but he couldn't make out the words.

"Ride out, follow me, and stay low," he instructed Cassidy, pulling her to her feet. As the horses galloped up, they swung into the saddles, Cassidy onto the Appaloosa. Fargo led on the Ovaro as they sped down the hill. Three bullets zinged just overhead and then they were careening down the trail. In the distance off to his left, he heard the shouts of the *bandidos*. No doubt they had caught up with the runaway bay and had discovered his ruse. The Ovaro and the Appaloosa were plummeting down the trail under the cottonwoods. They would have to make great speed and try to get back to the safety of the ranch before the gang caught up with them.

All the while they rode under the trees and then out onto the barren land under the stars, Fargo wondered if he was doing the right thing. What was it that Diego had said to Cassidy? You think you can own everything, he had said to her. Now just what was that supposed to mean? He'd find out from Cassidy when they got back to the ranch.

The horses galloped full out as the miles flew by beneath their pounding hooves, and despite the cool desert night air, sweating foam flecked their coats. In an hour's time they had reached the boundary of the ranch. Fargo had kept an eye out behind them and was surprised there was no sign of pursuit.

As they neared the dilapidated compound, a warning shot rang out overhead, followed by a shout. Cassidy shouted back to identify themselves. The ranch hands emerged from hiding places around the compound. The Flying D was like an armed camp, ready for attack.

They dismounted and the ranch hands gathered around excitedly. Cormac O'Neill stood apart, glowering as usual. The ranch hands all wanted to know what had happened.

While Cassidy was telling them, Fargo led the Ovaro to the watering trough and rubbed down the sweating, tired horse as it drank and ate a few oats. He stabled the horse. No one had made a move to take care of the Appaloosa, so he did that too, then returned to the group just as Cassidy was finishing her story.

"And that's how Mr. Fargo got us away from them," Cassidy said. "Thanks to the sheep and the thorns."

"So are we going to attack their hideout tonight?" one ranch hand asked eagerly.

"Diego knows our plan," Fargo said. "Without the element of surprise, it would be a losing battle. We'll have to think of something else. We were just damned lucky to get away. But our luck may not hold if Diego makes an assault on this place. Now, Cassidy, just what did he mean when he accused you of wanting to own everything in the valley?"

She gazed at him blankly. Then a troubled look crossed her face and she seemed to suppress it quickly, as if trying to hide her thoughts.

"You know," she said impatiently to him, "it's like I told you before. Diego Segundo wants a piece of everything we transport in or out of Corazon. He thinks it's his right to take a little from everybody. And I just won't stand for it. I've got a ranch to run here."

She turned and walked quickly toward the ranch house and once again Fargo was certain she wasn't telling the whole truth.

A few hours later, morning came on quick, a flash of gold-white in the east that changed to burning white as the sun's orb ascended the pale blue cloudless sky.

During the night, Fargo had managed to catch a few hours' sleep on a pile of hay in the barn. The ranch hands had been convinced Diego would try something and they sat up all night waiting for an attack that never came. Fargo had been pretty sure Diego wouldn't opt for an all-out assault, but he couldn't convince the hands of that. During the day, the ranch was easy to defend because you could see somebody coming for miles. But at night they might sneak up on you. This is what the ranch hands were afraid of. He had tried to talk them into leaving two or three men on guard and sending the rest for a good night's sleep. After all, they'd need to be fit in the morning. But instead, the ranch hands quarreled over who would keep watch and all of them ended up waiting through the long night, rifles at the ready.

So as the morning light spilled across the dusty yard, the ranch hands were dozing at their lookout points. Cassidy was inside the ranch house and Fargo was giving the Ovaro a thorough curry when he glanced up and saw a dark smudge, a horseman approaching far away. His keen eyes searched the horizon all around. There was nobody else. The man was alone. And somehow he knew it was not one of Diego's men. A few minutes later, one of the men who was supposedly doing guard duty spotted the approaching stranger. He called out to the others and they all came running and stood around with raised rifles as the lone rider came into the compound.

"Is this the Flying D Ranch?" the short man asked, looking around at all the armed men.

"Sure is."

"I got a message for Miz Cassidy Donohue."

One of the hands went inside the ranch house to

wake her up. She emerged a few minutes later bleary-eyed and stumbling. Fargo wondered if she'd been drinking before she went to sleep.

"I'm Thaddeus Perkin from the Santa Fe Shipping Company," the man announced when Cassidy introduced herself. "Please'd to meet you, m'am. I'm supposed to come tell you in person that your shipment is coming down from the States. It's early by a week. Left Chihuahua yesterday." He sounded very proud.

"What? But that can't be! It's not supposed to arrive until next week!" Cassidy sounded panicky.

"Well, it's a-coming," said Perkin stolidly. "We get our shipments there on time or even earlier. It's ready for pickup tomorrow morning at the turnoff to the Blue Sierras right on the Chihuahua Trail. Our men will hold the wagons there till you get your men in place to bring it through the mountains. That was the deal, wasn't it?"

"No! Goddamn it! I won't accept this," Cassidy said. "I'm not ready to receive that shipment yet. We've got *bandido* troubles in the hills right now. Can't you understand that? And I've got to wipe them out once and for all. Before that shipment comes into this valley. Hold the shipment in Chihuahua until I'm ready. I can't, I can't." Cassidy was sounding hysterical.

"Sorry, m'am," Thaddeus Perkin said. "I can't do that. Your shipment is going to be there waiting for you tomorrow morning, ready for collection. Now unless you want me to send it back to the States—"

"No, no." Cassidy seemed thoughtful. Perkin gave exact instructions where the Santa Fe Shipping Company would be waiting with the wagons. And then he prepared to ride off, his duty done.

"I have a question," Fargo cut in. "Did you come over the Sangre Pass to get through the Blue Sierras?"

"Sure," Perkin said. "That's the only way I know in and out of this valley."

"Did you encounter any trouble?" Fargo asked.

"Damn right I did," Perkin snapped. "You know damn well I got stopped by that fellow's gang of thieves. Had to pay them fifty dollars just to get past. Of course I didn't tell 'em anything about the shipment. And that's the reason I told 'em I was a patent medicine salesman." He pulled up a flap on his saddlebag and removed a blue glass vial. "And that's exactly why we don't deliver anything all the way to this valley. Nobody will. And also why I couldn't just send a message on paper. Had to come myself. So, Miz Cassidy, you just send some of your men by there tomorrow. But good luck getting by that *bandido*."

Thaddeus Perkin tipped his hat, his duty done. He rode out and Cassidy watched him go, fury in her face.

"No, no," she muttered to herself. "I won't have this happen."

"Look, there's not much you can do right now," Fargo said. "Why don't you just pay some of the shipment to Diego while we figure out how to stop him in the future."

"No!" Cassidy said, her voice stone hard. "That shipment must arrive at this ranch completely untouched. Do you understand?" Fargo wondered again what could be so blasted valuable or important that she couldn't spare any bit of it. Suddenly, she softened, as if realizing how harshly she'd been speaking.

"Trust me, Skye," she said. "And please, please agree to help me. I need you now. More than ever." She turned the charm up full blast, blinking her green eyes at him and running her hand through her red hair as if the responsibilities of the ranch had suddenly become all too much for her to handle and she needed him, desperately needed him, to help.

But he knew Cassidy was putting on an act, playing for his sympathy. And for now, he pretended to go along with it. He was going to get to the bottom of this once and for all. And in his experience you could only get to the bottom of things by diving right in.

"Sure, I'll help you," he said agreeably. "Just what do you want me to do?"

"Lead the expedition to retrieve that shipment," Cassidy said. "And bring it back to me here at the ranch. Please find a way to take those goods over the Blue Sierras so Diego doesn't even know you're there, doesn't get his hands on it. I need those . . . those supplies for the winter. Otherwise, I'm going to lose this ranch."

"Sure," Fargo said. "I'll try."

Cassidy appointed some of her men to accompany Fargo. She included Cormac among them. Fargo started to protest and then thought better of it. Let her think she was totally in charge.

Two hours later, Fargo led ten of the ranch hands on horseback out of the compound. They were a motley bunch. The hotheaded Cormac was about the most competent of them all. Fargo realized that in a pitched gunfight, these ten cowpokes were sure to lose against more than two dozen of Diego's well-trained gang. But he had to see the job through now, had to figure out what it was all about.

And he knew he'd have to run into Diego Segundo again. Besides somebody in the gang had his trusty Colt pistol.

7

The next morning, Fargo sat on the Ovaro, looking down at the Chihuahua Trail. Ten of Cassidy's ranch hands sat on horses behind him. It had been a damned hard drive through the mountains all the previous day and through the night. They had circled far out from the village of Corazon before entering the highlands. And once into the hills, he'd led them on a zigzag course through obscure passes and over the summits of tall peaks. Anything to make sure that Diego and his gang wouldn't be able to follow.

And now below them were three wagons of supplies bound for the Flying D Ranch. The men who worked for the Santa Fe Shipping Company stood waiting and watching warily as they descended the slope. As soon as they reached the bottom, Fargo hailed them and recognized the short man, Thaddeus Perkin, who had come to the Flying D Ranch the day before.

"Well, you got here all right," the short man said, beaming. "It's all yours now, wagons, mule teams, and supplies. Now, we'll just get a move on." He nervously scanned the barren hills around them, clearly imagining that Diego Segundo and his gang would be swooping down on them at any moment. The men of the Santa Fe Shipping Company mounted and rode out with hardly a backward glance.

Cormac tethered his horse and sprinted around to the back of a wagon, followed by several of the other ranch hands. Fargo watched them curiously. Something seemed to be up. He dismounted and followed, only to find them gathered in a circle and looking in at the contents of the wagon. They were whispering, but as soon as they spotted him they shut up. Fargo pushed them aside and glanced into the back of the wagon, curious to see this all-important shipment. It wasn't much to look at. Long narrow wooden crates were stamped FOOD. The tubby barrels were marked FLOUR.

"All right, unload these wagons," Fargo ordered. "And unhitch the mules."

"Unload?!" Cormac said indignantly. "But that's a couple hours' work! Why don't we just drive these wagons back to the ranch? You can't just order us around like that. I promised Cassidy I'd—" Cormac stopped himself, his face coloring.

"You'd what?" Fargo shot at him. When he didn't answer, Fargo addressed all the men gathered there. "You're going to pull these barrels and crates out of these wagons. Then unhitch the mule teams and tie the goods on to each mule."

"Why can't we leave 'em in the wagons?" one of the men asked.

"We'll never get these lumbering wagons through the mountains without Diego finding us," Fargo snapped. "There's only one wagon trail, Sangre Pass, through the mountains, remember? And Diego's got that locked up tight."

"I thought the famous Trailsman was supposed to be able to find new trails," Cormac taunted. "Including wagon trails."

"Get the wagons unloaded," Fargo repeated with an edge of exasperation. "Now, Cormac. And the rest of you get moving. You two stand guard up on the hill and keep your eyes open for anybody approaching. We don't want to get ambushed before we even hit the trail."

The men fell to work stacking the big barrels and crates beside the trail. They unhitched the mules and roped the goods to the pack animals, balancing them carefully. Even heavily loaded, the surefooted mules could climb the most rugged trails. It would be much easier to slip a line of mules invisibly through the mountains than a bunch of squeaking, ponderous mountain wagons.

As the last mule was being loaded, Fargo wondered again just why Cassidy thought she could save her entire ranch by ordering food supplies for another year. It seemed to him that she was just putting off the inevitable. The ranch didn't have enough water to raise cattle on. Or even sheep, for that matter. And yet she was holding on to the hope of this one shipment getting through. It just didn't make sense.

At last, Fargo directed the men to drag the empty wagons to the side of the road. They prepared to ride out. The day was bright but rain clouds were gathering in the west, piling towers on towers, higher and higher. In the distance, the sparkling anvil head of a gigantic thundercloud was taking shape. It might be a wet afternoon.

At Fargo's signal, the long mule train moved up the steep slope and over the first rise, heading through the twisted high country of the Blue Sierras. He led the way, picking routes that would keep them low down and as hidden as possible. Ever since he had arrived in the Blue Sierras, it had struck him that Diego Segundo seemed to have eyes everywhere, seemed to know who was moving across twisted land. He recalled how Diego had known exactly when the shipment was coming up the Chihuahua Trail. Just how did he do that? The sun came and went as the clouds scudded by.

In midafternoon, he was riding along a narrow rocky trail when he spotted a flash on a peak far ahead of him. He stared at the spot and then saw it again, distinctly, a bright pinpoint flash, like . . . like the reflection of the sun in a small mirror, he thought. Yes, that was how Diego did it! He remembered Diego climbing to the top of a nearby hill just before the ambush. He had probably been getting a signal about the exact location of the wagon train. That's how he was able to time it so exactly. Diego's gang had developed some kind of code, and with the reflective mirrors they could keep each other informed over vast distances, from mountain peak to mountain peak. It was ingenious. But, he realized, it was also dangerous. What he had just seen was one of Diego's men sending a signal. They'd been spotted.

Fargo looked up and saw that the clouds were beginning to thicken. With luck, there would be no more direct sun and Diego's gang would not be able to send any more signals about the mule train's whereabouts. But even now it might be too late. He considered the terrain and the sky and decided to make an evasive maneuver, hoping Diego's riders might miss them altogether. He drove the mules hard to the left suddenly, up over a hillside, and plunging down into a valley and another track that led up a rocky canyon and climbed up and over another mountain saddle. Of course, if Diego ran across their trail, it would be pretty easy to follow. But there were hundreds of square miles out here. And the sky was now lowering with black clouds. If the rain fell hard enough to obliterate their tracks, then Diego might be searching for him blindly this afternoon, without the mirror signals. Just maybe they'd get lucky.

"Where the hell are we going?" Cormac O'Neill came riding up alongside him. "Looks to me like we're lost. I don't think you know where you're going. As of now, I'm going to take over this mule train."

Fargo ignored him, focusing on the trail up ahead where it forked. The right-hand trail led along the top of a cliff and disappeared over a saddle. The left fork appeared more distinct and easier to negotiate, a narrow passage of a gently sloping trail through a ravine with walls of tumbled scree that seemed to go straight on for a long way. Small pebbles were everywhere, gray as the rock faces of the towering peaks high overhead, gray as the threatening sky. He heard the rumble of thunder and the first few drops of rain spattered the rocks.

He didn't like the look of the left fork. Not at all. Something told him to bear right and he started heading that way. To his surprise, Cormac pulled his mount about and defiantly took the left fork and motioned for the rest of the mule train to follow. The man leading the first mules hesitated only an instant, then followed Cormac. The rain began to fall more steadily. Lightning cracked far overhead, followed by a clap of thunder.

"What the hell do you think you're doing?" Fargo shouted after them.

"I'm getting this shipment back to the ranch like I said I would," said Cormac.

There was nothing he could say or do to dissuade the Flying D ranch hands. They were following Cormac and smirking at Fargo as they passed by. Fargo swore and brought up the rear. Hell, he didn't like this trail. High above them, the walls of tumbled rock looked down on them. It was a damned perfect place for an ambush. No way to escape. And a man would hardly get a clear shot at his attackers. As the rain continued to fall in sheets of gray, they traveled two miles between the slopes of talus. Suddenly, above the hiss of the rain he heard something. The whinny of a horse up ahead. He called a halt, passing the word up the mule train.

"What's going on?" Cormac shouted back at him, peering around behind.

"Trouble," Fargo said. "Get ready for an ambush."

Fargo pulled the Henry rifle out of the saddle

scabbard, grateful that even though Diego had his Colt pistol, he'd neglected to remove the rifle from the Ovaro's saddle the night they'd been captured. The rain began to ease up, the gray clouds scudding fast over the tall peaks.

His keen eyes swept the gray rocky slopes, the narrow defile. Yeah, they'd ridden right into it, damn it, but there was no helping it. Suddenly, there they were. Diego Segundo's men appeared from over the top of the ridge high above them. Their rifle barrels pointed downward into the narrow ravine. They were goddamn sitting ducks.

It only took a split second for Cormac and the rest of the men to realize their position. In a panic, the men dismounted, shouting frantically. They pulled the horses and mules down and tried to take cover behind the animals. Meanwhile, Fargo slipped down off the Ovaro and slapped it away out of the line of fire. It reluctantly retreated down the trail. He pulled his knife out and sliced through the ropes on the two nearest mules, so the barrels and crates fell to the ground. He drove the mules off and threw himself down under cover behind the crates just as the bullets began to rain in on them.

Fargo fired upward, barely missing the *bandidos* who were hidden there up above him. It was an impossible fight with terrible odds. Diego and his men were occupying the high ground on both sides of the ravine, while Fargo and the ranch hands of the Flying D were trapped at the very bottom.

The bullets were whining and ricocheting all around him. He aimed the Henry and pulled the trigger, saw one of Diego's men sink down behind a rock, a bullet hole in his forehead. He fired five more times, then reloaded. Up above, the *bandidos* were reloading for every shot, but they kept up a pretty steady rain of bullets. The ranch hand ahead of him screamed in agony and writhed on the ground, holding his leg. Then another hail of bullets came in and the ranch hand jerked and didn't move again. Some of the others were crying out in agony. As he popped up and looked up the trail, he could see several dead men sprawled out and others, badly wounded, making a last-ditch stand.

Hell, maybe he could get Diego to make a deal and stop all the killing. It was worth a try. It was a slaughter and they could remain hopelessly pinned down. Suddenly Fargo realized that none of the *bandidos* were aiming at him. They were shooting Cassidy's men, but they seemed to be leaving him alone. Was it orders from Diego? If so, maybe it gave him just the chance he was looking for. Fargo leapt to his feet, raised his arms, and shouted out to them.

"Are you crazy?" Cormac shouted back at him. "Get under cover, you damn fool!"

The clatter of gunfire slowed, then ceased.

"Diego!" Fargo called out. "Let's talk. Make a deal. Tell me what you want."

"NO!" The bullet whined right beside his head, barely missing him. It had come from Cormac O'Neill's single-shot rifle.

"What the hell was that?" Fargo shouted at Cormac.

"No deal with Diego!" he yelled as he reloaded.

Fargo pulled up the barrel of his Henry. He hated to do this, but he had no choice. Cormac brought the barrel of his single-shot rifle up again. In a split second, Fargo took aim at the tall black barrel waving almost straight up in the air and squeezed the trigger six times in close succession as the ravine rang with explosions. Cormac's rifle barrel had been hit by the bullets and splintered.

Fargo heard a howl of rage as Cormac realized he was weaponless. Suddenly, despite the *bandidos* hiding up above them, Cormac jumped to his feet and stumbled in a blind passionate fury back toward Fargo, hurtling over the dead bodies and past his wounded companions, bent on revenge. Fargo saw him coming and rose from behind the crates, throwing down his Henry. Yeah, they'd have it out now, he and Cormac, hand to hand.

Without a word, Cormac came on, his pale eyes gleaming with a death wish, his face flushed with fury, his fists hard balls of sinew. Cormac's passion and desperation gave him an almost superhuman strength. The first blow, a sizzling arc, took Fargo by surprise, catching him in the jaw. He staggered backward and stars danced across the scene.

Cormac moved in again, delivering a powerful left, and Fargo felt his organs shift around painfully. He stumbled and rallied, got a half-delivered left to Cormac's belly, followed by a bone-crunching right under the jawline. Cormac's head snapped upward and he sank to his knees. Fargo threw himself on top of him and they rolled over and over on the rocks, raining blows on one another.

"You . . . goddamn . . . fucking . . . bastard,"

Cormac grunted between blows. "Keep . . . away . . . from . . . Cassidy."

Fargo delivered a breathtaking punch to the midsection that shut Cormac up for a while. He gasped for air like a drowning fish and his eyes rolled in his head.

"You can have the bitch," Fargo spat.

That brought Cormac around again. With a wail, he became a pummeling machine, his meaty fists driven as if by rotaries, connecting again and again with powerful, bruising blows. Fargo felt his right eye swell shut and his right side was stabbing with pain. A few broken ribs, he guessed.

"To hell with you, Cormac," Fargo said.

The black rage rose in him then, a hot flow of liquid strength to his arms, powerful chest, and his legs. He felt the power surge in him as he leapt to his feet, hauling Cormac by the collar. He aimed a right square into his face and smashed it for all he was worth. Cormac went limp and fell like a sack of potatoes onto the rocks, hitting his head. For a moment, Fargo thought he was dead and he knelt beside the bloodied Irishman. But he was still breathing. He'd be out for a good long while though.

Fargo stood. Everything hurt and he tasted blood in his mouth from a deep split lip. He could hardly see out of one eye and the earth moved like ocean waves under his feet. He staggered and barely managed to keep his balance.

"Good fighting, Fargo." Diego called down.

"So, how about it? Let's have a talk. I'm sure we can come to an agreement."

"Disarm those men first," Diego said. "I do not trust them. Then I will come down."

Fargo moved from man to man and wrested their battered rifles from them. Three were willing to give them up. Two protested, but then gave in. In addition to Cormac, there were only five ranch hands left alive. Fargo threw the rifles down in a pile and told the remaining men to sit in a row beside the trail.

"Those Mexican bastards will shoot us in the backs!" one protested.

"If you don't do it, they'll shoot you anyway," Fargo snapped. They dragged themselves over to the rocks and sat down.

"All clear!" Fargo called out.

Diego and a few of his men ventured down the slope tentatively, their rifles ready. When they reached the bottom, the men took positions guarding the ranch hands. Diego took Fargo's arm.

"You remember I like a man who can tell such good lies," Diego said with a laugh. "But I do not understand you, Señor Fargo. Is it just that you will do anything you are paid to do? Is that it?"

Fargo wondered at Diego's words. What was he driving at?

"Look, Diego. I think you and Cassidy Donohue need to sit down and negotiate some kind of treaty. She says all she wants is to get these supplies so her ranch can get through the winter. You've seen the Flying D Ranch. They've got no water. She's holding on by her fingernails out there."

Diego stared at him in disbelief and his face slowly darkened.

"Now you are telling bad lies, Señor Fargo. You think maybe I am stupid? This I cannot tolerate. For this, you must die."

Diego Segundo suddenly brought the barrel of his rifle up and pointed it straight between Fargo's eyes. Fargo stared down the long barrel into the blazing eyes of the *bandido*. And in those eyes he saw hatred, fear, and revenge.

"*Sí*. You must die now, Trailsman."

"Stop! Stop it!"

A woman's voice, Rita's voice calling out over the clatter of horses' hooves on the tumbling slope of scree. Fargo and Diego looked up in surprise to see Rita on horseback, sliding down the slope, her hair wild around her. She was followed close behind by one of Diego's men. They reined in and dismounted. Rita ran toward them and threw herself in front of Fargo.

"You can't do this, Diego."

"What is Rita doing here?" Diego demanded of the man. "I sent you to the cantina to guard over her in case of trouble."

"She said she would shoot herself if I did not bring her to where you were," the man said, hanging his head. Diego stamped his foot and raised his rifle, pointing it at Rita.

"Step away from him. He must die."

"No, Diego. He is innocent. He doesn't know."

"He is lying!"

"No, Diego. I heard Señora Donohue talking to him. She did not tell him. He does not know."

"Know what?" Fargo cut in. "What the hell is going on?"

In answer, Diego drew a knife from his belt and leaned down to pull the top off one of the wooden crates. Fargo expected to see canned goods and other foodstuffs inside. Instead, he saw stacks of rifles. The most up-to-date repeating Henry rifles like his own. A rare commodity in Mexico. And there were a lot of them. He looked at all the wooden crates littering the trail and whistled low. A helluva lot of rifles.

"And the barrels are full of gunpowder," Diego said.

"What was she going to do with all those guns? Start a war?"

"After she wiped out our hideout, she planned to massacre the whole town of Corazon," Diego said. "She wanted the land, you see. The land with water. There is not enough land with water for everyone to have some in the valley of Corazon."

Fargo looked over the crates of rifles again. Compared to the guns he had seen in the hands of Diego's men and on the ranch, these new rifles shot further, were more accurate, and could shoot six times before reloading. With such superior firepower, Cassidy Donohue was sure to win every gunfight.

"Is this true?" Fargo asked one of the ranch hands sitting in the row being watched over by several of Diego's men. The hands nodded guiltily.

It all made sense now. Cassidy Donohue had to get the rifles into the valley by a secret path. Because if Diego ambushed the shipment he would discover them and do more than simply take his usual tribute. And no wonder when Diego got wind that the famous Skye Fargo was coming to help make it all possible, he tried to get him killed.

Right now, Cassidy Donohue and the rest of her ranch hands were waiting at the Flying D Ranch for the shipment of guns to arrive so they could begin the slaughter and the land grab. He walked over and picked up one of the new Henry rifles from the open crate, sighting along the barrel. Yeah, she'd just about managed it too, the bitch.

"So Cassidy Donohue double-crossed you too," Diego said, coming to stand next to him.

"Damn right," Fargo muttered. "And she sure took me in with that story of how those rich landowners back in Ireland took everything for themselves. She's come to this country and she's trying to do the same thing herself. Only this time she's the one doing the taking." He swore a few more oaths.

"But as long as she is in Corazon, she will try to take over the land."

"Right. And the Flying D Ranch is like an armed camp right now," Fargo said. "She and her men are dug in there and it would take a whole troop to roust 'em. So, I've got another idea," he said. Diego's eyes glittered as he started to tell him what he had in mind.

"*Sí*, is a very good plan," Diego said. "We do that." Suddenly Fargo felt a hand on his arm and Rita was standing beside them.

"Good thing I come to save you, Skye." Her

dark eyes were laughing. "Or else my brother would have killed you for sure. But now I see you and Diego are like old friends."

"Brother?" Fargo puzzled over that. "Diego is your brother?" She shrugged and nodded. "But what about Alonzo?"

"Brother also. Diego and Alonzo are brothers," Rita said. Diego, hearing Alonzo's name, spat on the ground and stomped off to oversee the tying up of the ranch hands. Fargo watched him go, trying to fit together the puzzle pieces.

"I heard you say it was Alonzo's fault that Diego is a *bandido*," Fargo said to Rita. "What did you mean by that?"

"Alonzo is older brother," Rita said. "When our father died, all the land and sheep went to him. There wasn't much, just enough for one man. But usually, the older brother divides the land with the other brothers. Alonzo said the land is too small, so he kept it all. Then Diego, he threw away the name Ramirez, named himself Segundo."

"It means . . . second, number two," Fargo said.

"*Sí*, number two son," Rita explained. "And Diego, he was so angry, he rode into the foothills and started this gang. Since then, they learn all the mountains, get many goods, and bring them to Corazon, become popular with all the people."

"And that makes Alonzo mad."

"Alonzo is afraid Diego will become so popular he will take the land away from him."

Fargo shook his head. The old quarrel between the two brothers seemed so senseless. And it was all because there wasn't enough water in the land, not enough sheep for every man to have a decent herd.

"What about the sheep that Diego is taking from Alonzo?"

"Sheep? Diego take sheep?" Rita shook her head. "I do not think so. Diego would never do that. We know the ranch hands are taking the sheep from the herders. They come at night and little by little, they take what they want."

"Well, the main thing now is to get Cassidy Donohue and her men out of the valley" Fargo said, speaking his thoughts out loud.

"We are ready now, Señor Trailsman?" Diego, having finished directing his men, came up rubbing his hands together. "Now we will finally take care of those Irish invaders. Ready?"

"Ready."

"One more thing." Diego handed over the Colt pistol. Fargo felt its familiar weight in his hand.

"Ready," he repeated.

It was just after midnight, the moon was rising and the night was turning cool, a stiff wind blowing across the high Blue Sierras.

"Hurry," Fargo called out to the men straggling behind. He turned about in his saddle to see the line of Cassidy Donohue's dozen men strung out behind them, riding under the shimmering cottonwood trees. Each of them was carrying a brand-new Henry rifle. He'd brought down one crate from the shipment, enough for each man to have one.

Cassidy had been surprised to see him ride into the ranch alone just after sunset, surprised he knew about the rifles and didn't seem to mind, even more surprised to hear his story. He told how the shipment had made it through the Blue Sierras safely. He told how he'd caught sight of Diego's gang and tracked them into their hideout. How he'd left Cormac watching over the entrance so he could ride to the ranch bringing some of the better rifles to arm the rest of the men.

"You think Diego and his men will still be in their hideout?" Cassidy asked. She was riding beside him. Her voice betrayed her excitement but he didn't hear a note of suspicion. "If so, we've got them trapped."

"Like rats in a hole," Fargo said. "Cormac's keeping watch. And all we have to do is ride up and pour some firepower into that canyon and we've got 'em."

He glanced over to see Cassidy Donohue's tight self-satisfied smile. No doubt about it, she was thinking how once she got the Diego gang wiped out and he left the valley, she'd turn those Henry rifles on the whole village of Corazon. And then the whole valley would be hers.

The trail began to climb up into the hills, slowly ascending.

"Hold together!" Fargo commanded. He slowed until the men bunched up behind him. They'd have to do this just right. It would all be in the timing. He slowed the line of men to a bare walk. They rode now with their rifles ready, poised and wary. The rocky path was winding through the hills now and the turnoff to Diego's hideout was just ahead.

"How far?"

"Almost there," he assured her. He reined in the Ovaro. "This is where we dismount and go on foot. I'll lead through this next stretch. It's a narrow entrance and it opens up to a cliff. Below will be Diego's hideout. We'll string out and get into position and then at my signal, get ready to shoot."

Cassidy Donohue's men nodded agreement eagerly, stroking the Henry rifles.

"Can't wait to use this baby," one of them muttered.

"Yeah, getting them loaded was pure pleasure. Helluva lot better than those one shots we've been totin'."

There was a shallow ravine just up ahead. Fargo glanced around. He knew there were some of Diego's men hidden in the nearby rocks but he couldn't spot them. They were good, damned good. He dismounted.

They hid the horses in a shallow ravine to one side of the trail. Fargo cautioned them to be quiet. He paused at the narrow entrance to the rock crevice and gathered Cassidy's men around him. She stood at his elbow. In the dim starlight he could see the grim faces.

"We'll have to go in one at a time," he said. "And don't make a sound. Diego's men won't be expecting us to sneak up this back way. When you come out of the rock, hunch down and take cover. When everybody's through, we'll attack."

"I don't like this," one of the ranch hands suddenly protested. "Where's Cormac anyhow?"

"He's keeping watch just inside," Fargo said.

He could feel Cassidy's eyes on him, the slight suspicion rising. "Cormac and the rest of the men have taken up good positions right over Diego's hideout. All we need to wipe out the gang is a few more good guns."

"We got those," one said, hefting the new Henry rifle.

"That's right," Fargo said. "So we'll go in and blast 'em."

"Yeah," a few muttered.

Fargo led the way with Cassidy close at his heels. She was gripping one of the rifles eagerly.

"Put your hand on my shoulder," he instructed. They slipped between the huge rocks, winding through the narrow passageway. Above, in the sliver of sky, the stars shone but deep in the rock, it was black as pitch. With one hand, he held the Colt before him. With the other, he brushed against the rock wall as he felt his way forward with his feet. The passageway made a sharp turn to the left and he pulled her along. The ranch hands were close behind and occasionally one stumbled and swore in the dark. Just ahead, dim starlight lit the open space, the round canyon that was Diego's hideout. He was counting on the men not being able to see in the darkness exactly where they were emerging until it was too late. And Diego's men were waiting to club the men over the head one by one as they came out. Fargo stepped out of the passageway into the starlight. He spotted the dark forms of Diego's men hunched down behind the rocks on either side.

Cassidy drew a sharp breath as the canyon

opened up before them, the small, round hideout with the stream glittering across its rocky floor. Before she could get a good look and give an alarm, Fargo pulled her sharply to one side, spun her about, and clapped his hand over her mouth. Her reaction was instantaneous and he could feel in the sudden stiffness of her small frame the realization she'd been betrayed. Her eyes were lit with fury as she struggled like a wildcat in his grip, biting the palm of his hand, scratching at his arm. Behind them, the first ranch hand emerged and two of Diego's men were on him instantly, knocking him out cold and dragging him away.

Seeing this, Cassidy fought all the harder in his grasp, brought the rifle around and tried to club him. With his free hand, he tried to stop her as she fumbled for the trigger. The rifle exploded but no bullet whined. Instead, the barrel blew up in a stinging burning roar of gunpowder and flash. The next man to appear at the entranceway ducked back before Diego's men could jump him. His rifle backfired and blew up in his hands. He shouted a warning to the rest of the men and gunfire clattered from within the narrow passageway as Cassidy's men realized something had gone wrong and panicked.

Cassidy renewed her struggle and jerked the useless rifle around, trying to hit him with it, but he caught it easily and held it up before her face with its busted barrel.

"That's right," he said into her ear as he held her hard against him. "Every one of the rifles I gave your men has a pebble jammed down hard into the barrel. And every one of them is going to backfire." The pop of gunfire was echoing off the rocks and Fargo knew that Diego's men were now sweeping in from behind, driving the ranch hands forward into the canyon. Fargo removed his hand from Cassidy's mouth.

"Fargo, you double-crossing bastard," she spat. "You've thrown in with that *bandido* Diego. When I'm out of here, I'm going to tell this story from here to Ogallala and your reputation is going to be dirt. You'll never get another trailing job as long as you live."

"Truth always comes out in the end. People have a way of figuring out who's telling lies," Fargo said. "You lied when you hired me. You told me you were waiting for food supplies and that you just wanted to save your ranch and keep Diego's gang from getting a stranglehold on the valley. All along, you were planning to kill everybody in Corazon and take over all the land. You lied and you're just getting your own back."

Cassidy subsided into silence and watched as her men were pushed one by one out of the passageway. Each of the confused and angry ranch hands held a busted Henry rifle in his hands. Diego came up and gave orders that Cormac and the five remaining men be brought out of the caves where they'd been hidden. The rest of Diego's men emerged too, along with Rita Ramirez. As he was led forward, Cormac spotted Cassidy being held by Fargo. With a hoarse cry, he broke loose and despite the fact that his arms were bound in front of him, he barreled toward them.

Fargo threw Cassidy to one side just before Cormac O'Neill hit him. They went down onto the rocky canyon floor, Cormac trying to roll on top of him.

"You . . . get . . . away . . . from her!" Cormac grunted.

In an instant, Fargo realized what was happening as he felt the Colt slip from his holster. Cormac had grabbed for it with his bound hands. They rolled over and over on the rocky ground, Cormac grunting with frustration as he tried to bring the pistol upward. Fargo reached down and gripped the barrel just as Cormac's finger found the trigger. The pistol roared, Cormac's body jolted and twitched. The acrid smell of gunsmoke filled the air. Fargo pulled his pistol from Cormac's hand and stood. The blond Irishman lay on his back, his eyes wide with fear, the blood darkening his chest. He had only moments to live.

"Cassidy!" She came to him then, knelt beside the man who had been her childhood friend and who had followed her across the ocean to try to help her start the ranch. "I love you, Cassidy." Cormac suddenly gave a deep sigh and his pale eyes went blank. Fargo leaned down and closed the lids.

"No," Cassidy said, disbelievingly. And in that one word Fargo heard realization and regret. Maybe she was just starting to understand that she had thrown away Cormac's loyalty and friendship and that because of her Cormac had died. He hoped it would haunt her for a long, long time. "Pa's gone. Cormac's gone. I'm all alone," she murmured.

"You should have thought of that sooner," he said. He hauled her roughly to her feet. "Let's get them all out of here," he called out to Diego. "Get this lot out of Corazon for good."

Dawn had gilded the sky when Cassidy and her remaining men had been readied for the trip out of the Blue Sierras. Diego and his men got them on their horses with a few days' supply of food in the saddlebags. A few of Diego's men would escort them as far as Chihuahua with the understanding that if any of them was ever spotted in the Blue Sierras again there would be a bullet without any questions asked.

Fargo stood with one arm around Rita Ramirez and watched as the line of horses began to move into the passageway. Cassidy Donohue turned and looked back at him, her face seemed torn with pain, but he wondered if she had learned her lesson. In a moment, she had disappeared along with the string of horses.

"Good riddance," Rita said.

"A good night's work," Diego laughed, punching Fargo in the arm.

Diego's men were lighting a campfire and the odor of coffee warmed the cool morning air. Fargo walked over to the spring to wash up. He knelt down beside where the cool water bubbled out between the rocks, at the base of the slope of scree, at the tiny spring that supplied the only water for the whole valley. He cupped his hands and dashed the sparkling water over his face and let it run down over his head and neck. Its clarity seemed to wash away everything about Cassidy, and the Flying D Ranch. Diego, kneeling beside him, drank a draft of the clear water.

Fargo heard a bird twitter with the coming of the light and listened to the pleasant splashing of the water, the deeper gurgle of the underground spring. Then he heard it, the darker sound as if a river were running underground, far beneath the rocks under his feet. It sounded as if there were a cavern underground where the water ran. Curious, he put his hand down between the wet rocks where the spring came from. He lifted aside some of them, then a few more. The water surged a little. Only a little—was it his imagination? He stood, tossed more rocks aside, thinking he'd been wrong.

"What are you doing?" Rita asked, coming to watch him. Diego stood looking on curiously.

Fargo lifted a larger rock away and a gush of water swelled the stream.

"What?" Diego saw it too. He hadn't been imagining it. Rita laughed, tucked up her skirts, and began to toss the smaller rocks away from the spring. The water rose. They caught the excitement of the rushing water and began to move more and more of the rocks away from the mouth of the spring. Fargo realized that sometime the spring had been stronger, but a rockslide had blocked some of the water from coming out to the surface and had diverted it back so that it had run deep inside the mountain.

Diego called over his men and in moments they were swarming over the wet rockslide, hauling away the rocks, shouting and laughing as the stream swelled. There was already twice as much water as there had been before. Fargo straightened up and stepped back to stand beside Rita and watch the men.

"I can't believe it! It's like a miracle!" She hugged him as Diego came up beside them. Already the small stream running across the floor of the canyon hideout had spilled over and was spreading across the rocks. Soon it would threaten the supplies packed into the caves and if it rose high enough, it would flood the whole canyon.

Fargo walked over to the lookout point and gazed down across the valley of Corazon. The morning light silvered the stream and he could see the rush of higher water swelling over the banks of the brook as it snaked down the mountains and across the flatlands below. Far into the distance, he knew the water was reaching its cool finger into the parched lands, past the trees that had died long ago in that sere territory that had been without water for many, many years. Rita and Diego came to stand beside him and to look down on the valley.

"You!" Diego called out to some of his men. "Pack the supplies onto the horses before the water will ruin them. *Sí, Sí!* Continue to remove the rocks! *Sí!* I know the hideout will be flooded." Diego turned and gazed across the valley of Corazon once more.

"I think it is time for me and my men to leave the Blue Sierras," he said to Fargo with a wink. He turned and went back to help his men.

"Now we have water, we will have peace," Rita

said. "You will . . ." she looked up at him shyly. "You will stay for a time in Corazon?"

"For a time," he said to her, his eyes on the distance, watching the silvery line of water as it advanced across the barren, empty land.

LOOKING FORWARD!
The following is the opening section from the next novel in the exciting *Trailsman* series from Signet:

THE TRAILSMAN #187
SIOUX WAR CRY

1861, northern Minnesota,
where bigotry raged like a wildfire,
blood rained in a downpour,
and the innocent were unwary victims . . .

Skye Fargo was about a mile out from Fort Snelling when the madwoman nearly killed him.

The big man with the steely lake blue eyes had stopped at noon to give the Ovaro a brief rest. They had been pushing hard for over a week, heading out before first light every morning and riding until late at night, and both of them were showing signs of fatigue. So when Fargo rounded a bend and saw a grassy clearing to the left of the trail, he reined up and allowed the Ovaro to graze.

The rutted excuse for a road was heavily used. Settlers had been streaming into the region ever since the federal government opened land west of the Mississippi River for settlement a few years back. Many lumberjacks were among them, bound for the growing new communities of Minneapolis and St. Anthony.

Several heavily laden wagons filled with noisy families, as well as occasional riders, passed Fargo as he sat propped against a stump, letting the sun warm him. The mornings were brisk in Minnesota at that time of year, and he welcomed the heat the afternoon would bring.

A knot of lumbermen leading pack mules had gone by a few minutes ago. In the quiet that followed, Fargo could hear a robin chirping in the pines behind him and chipmunks chattering in a nearby cluster of boulders. Overhead, a flock of ducks winged westward.

Fargo smiled. The sights and sounds of the wilderness never failed to have a soothing effect on him, and he felt his tense muscles relaxing. He was as much at home in the deep woods as most men were in a city or town.

Reaching up to push his hat brim back, Fargo suddenly froze. His skin prickled as it sometimes did when he was being observed by unseen eyes. Instinctively, he swiveled toward the bend.

Astride a fine bay sat a lanky man dressed in a black frock coat and a wide-brimmed black hat, the sort of garb favored by riverboat gamblers and the like. But no gambler alive had ever been able to ride up close to Fargo unnoticed. It was a feat worthy of an Apache or Sioux warrior.

Fargo studied the man closely while being studied in turn. Whereas he had a beard, the stranger was clean-shaven. Whereas his dark mane of hair fell to his shoulders, the stranger's sandy hair had been cropped close and trimmed around the ears. Dark eyes met his evenly.

"Howdy," the man said in a voice as deep as Fargo's own. "You wouldn't happen to know how much farther it is to Minneapolis, would you?"

"A mile or so," Fargo answered, resting his right hand on his thigh, close to his Colt.

The corners of the stranger's thin lips quirked upward. "Not the trusting type, are you, friend?"

Fargo shook his head. "I find that I live longer that way. "In these parts too much trust can get a man killed."

"I know what you mean." The stranger's grin widened. Reminds me of my grandfather's favorite saying." He paused. "Love thy neighbor, but never go anywhere without your gun."

Despite himself, Fargo laughed. His intuition told him that the man in black posed no threat. Yet at the same time he was sure there was a lot more to the rider than met the eye. The next moment the man shifted to squint up at the sun and the frock coat parted. Around the rider's waist was a wide red sash. Jutting from the top of it, butt forward, was a pearl-handled, ivory-plated Remington. "Nice pistol you have there."

"It hits what I aim at," the stranger allowed. Kneeing the bay forward, he said, "Well, nice meeting you. If you stop in Minneapolis and don't mind losing at cards, look me up. My name is Ethan Lee."

"If I do, I won't be the one who loses," Fargo said.

Lee found that amusing. "I respect a gent with confidence, even if he is a mite misguided." Touching his hat brim, he applied his spurs and was soon lost to view around the next turn to the north.

Fargo settled back to rest. The creak of wagon wheels in dire need of grease and the snorts of a plodding team heralded new arrivals. Presently another family of settlers appeared. Husband and wife were perched on the seat, both wearing homespun clothes that had seen better days. In the wagon was their raucous brood, five or six kids from the sound of things, all of them yelling and squealing and bickering at once.

The husband, a burly specimen who appeared as strong as one of his oxen, spied the clearing and veered toward it. "Hello there!" he hollered to be heard above the racket. "Hope you don't mind if we stop here a spell. My animals are tuckered out, and we need to stretch our legs."

Fargo could take a hint. Sighing, he rose and said, "Feel free. I was just leaving anyway." He walked to the Ovaro as the wagon rattled to a stop. Six grubby faces poked out and peered at him.

"It isn't far to Minneapolis, is it?" the husband inquired hopefully.

"Someone should post a sign," Fargo muttered, stepping into the stirrups.

"Pardon?"

"No, not far at all," Fargo revealed. "You'll be there within the hour." He glanced at the weary team and saw the top of an iron stove mixed in with the belongings crammed into the bed. "Maybe two, as filled as you are."

The husband let out with a howl of pure delight. "Did you hear that, Maude? We're almost there! After three whole months, we're almost to our new home!"

Yips of delights burst from the children. The man went on howling like a demented wolf as Fargo swung toward the trail. They were making so much noise that he did not realize another wagon was coming up behind them until it swept around the bend. He looked up just as it appeared and saw four lathered mules flying toward him at breakneck speed, being lashed on by a figure who flicked a bullwhip in cracking cadence.

"Out of the way, you damned idiot!" the figure bawled, making no attempt to stop or swerve.

The settler's wife screamed. So did several of her children.

Fargo hauled on the reins for all he was worth, cutting the pinto to the right to get out of the way. Normally steady of nerves and as dependable as gold, the Ovaro shied, rearing and plunging. The team flew past. It missed them by the width of a whisker, the rumbling of the wheels like the peal of thunder. Fargo glimpsed a beaming face, a shapely form in buckskins, and streaming red tresses.

Maybe it was being caught unaware by the

Ovaro. Maybe it was the shock of seeing the driver was a woman. Or maybe it was both combined that caused Fargo to suffer a mishap he rarely did. He was thrown.

The sky and the ground exchanged places. Trees were abruptly upside down. His hat went one direction and he went another. Then Fargo thudded onto his left shoulder, grimacing at pain that seared down his arm and spine. Dazed, he rolled onto his back and saw clouds spinning above him. Dimly, he heard footsteps rushing to his side. Grubby faces replaced the clouds.

"Stand back, kids! Give me room!" the settler bellowed.

Strong hands helped Fargo to sit up. He winced, his left shoulder tingling.

"Are you all right, mister?" the settler's wife asked, genuinely concerned. "I was afraid you'd split your skull open."

"That was a freight wagon," the husband noted, coughing as the cloud of dust raised by its passage wafted down over them. "Going like a bat out of hell, too."

"Harvey!" Maude said. "Watch your language when the children are present."

The settler was too excited to heed. "Did you see that female on top handle that whip of hers? Damn, she could make it sing!"

Someone placed Fargo's hat on his head, and he was boosted erect. His head clearing, he saw the Ovaro standing quietly now, head hung low as if ashamed of its antics. Fargo shrugged himself clear and straightened. "Thanks for the help," he said, anger swelling within him like the wind in a rising storm. Stalking to the stallion, he quickly mounted, jabbed his spurs into its flanks, and was off like a cannon shot, galloping hard in pursuit.

It galled Fargo that the woman had nearly ridden him down. They were a notorious lot, the freighters. Tough, rowdy, and as arrogant as the day was long, most acted as if roads had been invented just so they could barrel down them at speeds no sane person would dare go.

The thick dust prevented Fargo from catching sight of his quarry. He went around the turn to the north, raced along a straight stretch hundreds of yards long, and on around the base of a low hill. Up ahead someone hollered. A horse whinnied and a string of lusty oaths told Fargo that someone else had suffered the same fate he had.

Sure enough, once past the next bend Fargo saw the man in black in the act of standing. Ethan Lee, flushed with anger, shook a fist in the air. Another flurry of curses were hurled at the redhead, who had already vanished. There was no sign of the bay.

Lee turned as the Ovaro approached. Brushing off his sleeves, he growled, "Hello again, friend. You won't believe this, but a hellcat on a freight wagon nearly just trampled me to death."

"I believe it," Fargo said, drawing in the rein. "She did the same thing to me."

"Really?" Lee's color deepened. "When I catch up with that woman, I'm going to strangle her with those red locks of hers." Sticking two fingers into his mouth, he uttered a piercing whistle. Soon, from out of the woods, trotted his horse, reins dangling. "It's downright embarrassing. She spooked my animal so bad, he threw me. That's never happened before."

"Then we have something else in common," Fargo disclosed. Lee looked at him, and suddenly, although Fargo could not quite say why, the pair of them were laughing heartily.

"I'd hate to be that hellcat's husband," Lee commented as he forked leather. "She probably cracks her whip over him as much as she does her mules."

They rode on side by side. Fargo did not push to catch up to the freighter. Now that his anger had subsided, there was no need. Minneapolis was not very big. He'd find the troublemaker soon enough.

Removing his bandanna, Fargo wiped dirt from his cheek and neck. He thought of the dispatch in his saddlebags, which was responsible for his being there, and wondered if the officer who sent it had been misinformed.

Captain Jim Beckworth was career army. A competent, dedicated soldier, he had worked his way up the ranks while stationed at a variety of frontier posts.

A year ago, while crossing the prairie, Fargo had stumbled on Beckworth's cavalry patrol trapped in a gully by a small band of marauding Arapaho. He had winged the leader of the war party, causing them to scatter. In gratitude Beckworth had treated Fargo to a night of whiskey, women, and bawdy times that left Fargo with the world's worst hangover. They had not seen each other since.

Eight days ago, out of the blue, a message had caught up with him in Denver. It had been short and to the point: "COME QUICK. SIOUX UPRISING FEARED. HUNDREDS MAY DIE WITHOUT YOUR HELP." It had been sent by Beckworth from Fort Snelling in Minnesota.

So far, though, Fargo had seen no sign of the Sioux, or any evidence of the other Indian tribes known to inhabit the region. None of the travelers and locals he met had expressed any worry about an uprising. Everything appeared to be tranquil.

As if Ethan Lee were privy to Fargo's thoughts, the gambler mentioned casually, "You haven't happened to come across any sign of the Sioux in your travels, have you? Down in St. Louis I heard tell that they've been making some trouble up this way." Lee plucked a sterling white handkerchief from his shirt pocket and commenced cleaning his face.

"No, I haven't," Fargo said.

Ethan Lee sighed. "I hope to hell the rumors aren't true. There will be the devil to pay if they ever go on the warpath. Especially if most of the federal troops are sent East, as the newspapers are saying they might be."

Fargo was familiar with the accounts. Trouble was brewing between northern states and southern states over the issue of slavery. Some experts were predicting it would lead to war. People living on the frontier were worried that if hostilities did break out, all government troops would be called back to deal with the crisis, leaving wilderness outposts vulnerable to attacks by hostile Indians.

"I didn't catch your handle, by the way," Lee commented.

Fargo told him. His name was fairly well known west of the Mississippi, so he was not surprised when the gambler responded with "Interesting" and let it go at that.

Presently they caught up with a party of loggers who were collecting horses that had scattered into the trees on either side of the road. A beefy man holding a bloody arm at his side spotted them and pointed toward Minneapolis. "Any chance of one of you fetching a sawbones for us? I've got a hurt arm, and my partner Ben broke his leg."

Propped against a Norway pine was a lean man whose pants had been sliced open to reveal the wound.

"What happened?" Fargo asked. As if he could not guess.

The logger's jaw muscles twitched. "We were taking some spare horses to our outfit southwest of here when Wagon Annie came racing on down the road. She came close to killing the both of us! One of these days that woman is going to go too far!"

"Wagon Annie? That's what she calls herself?"

Ethan Lee said, and chuckled. "If she's such a nuisance, why doesn't someone put her in her place?"

"Are you crazy?" the logger said. "That female doesn't take guff off of anyone. Just try to trim her feathers, and she's liable to gut you or peel your skin off an inch at a time with that nasty whip of hers. She's as mean as a stuck snake when she's riled."

"Any woman can be tamed if a man puts his mind to it," Lee asserted.

Fargo knew differently, but he held his tongue. Any man who regarded women as if they were pets had a lot to learn about the female of the species. Some were as wild as mustangs, as willful as grizzlies, and no amount of "taming" was ever going to change them.

"Excuse me," interrupted the logger with the broken leg, "but while you two chuckleheads are jawing away, I'm suffering over here. How about that doctor? I'd like to get the bone reset before the end of the year."

Fargo lifted his reins, prepared to volunteer, but the gambler beat him to it.

"I'll go" Lee said, breaking into a trot. Over his shoulder he called back, "Nice meeting you, Skye. If we run into each other in town, the drinks will be on me."

Two more loggers came out of the woods, leading horses. They hurried to their stricken companion, one bringing a blanket to spread over him. Since they had the matter well in hand, Fargo rode on. It was not long before he encountered more travelers, including four wagons loaded with settlers. At the rate people were pouring into that region, it wouldn't be long before the Indians were crowded out.

Was that why the Sioux were agitated? Fargo asked himself. It was a pattern repeated again and again, ever since the first colonists had come to America. In their never ending quest for land, whites were slowly but surely forcing the Indians into a literal corner.

Years ago there had been savage warfare in New England and in the southeast part of the country due to this very thing. Now some were of the opinion that more bloodshed could erupt at any time in the West.

Fargo would hate to see that happen. Both sides would suffer terribly, the Indians worst of all. He did not share the commonly held view that the only good Indian was a dead one. In his estimation they deserved the same fair treatment as everyone else.

Presently the Ovaro crested a rise. Below unfolded a lush vista of verdant land crisscrossed by winding waterways. On the east side of the broad Mississippi River was St. Anthony, started by a missionary explorer many years before. On the west side was newer Minneapolis, and Fargo was amazed at how much it had grown since the last time he crossed the territory.

South of Minneapolis stood Fort Snelling. Built on an ideal site, near where the Mississippi and the Minnesota rivers met, one end was flanked by a steep hill for extra protection. As thirsty and hungry and tired as Fargo was, he headed for the fort first instead of the town.

The gate was wide open, and neither of the sentries challenged him. Nor did the soldiers manning the battlements raise a cry. Apparently, anyone was free to come and go as they pleased, so long as they were white. A Winnebago who tried to enter in front of Fargo was turned sternly away.

As military posts went, Snelling had more to offer than most. Officers' quarters were comfortable, the barracks for the enlisted men well insulated against the harsh winter climate. Provisions were seldom scarce thanks to a steady stream of river and freight traffic. Compared to some forts farther west, it was a paradise.

Fargo asked at the adjutant's office about his friend and learned the captain was at the officers' mess. A private was assigned to guide him. It being the middle of the afternoon, few officers were there. Fargo spied Beckworth at a table near the front with another officer. Both were so engrossed in their talk that neither were aware of him until the private snapped to attention and announced crisply, "Colonel Williams, sir! A visitor to see the captain."

Jim Beckworth was a broad-shouldered man with a thick mustache. He leaped out of his chair and clapped Fargo on the arms as he might a long-lost relative. "Skye! You received my message! Thank God you came!"

Fargo had the dispatch in his right hand. Wagging it, he said with a smile, "This had better be important. I was on a winning streak when it reached me."

The captain swung toward his superior, a portly man who had risen and was smoothing his gray-flecked hair. "Colonel, allow me to introduce the fellow I was telling you about, the only one who can avert the bloodshed we foresee."

Fargo and Williams shook. The private was dismissed. A fresh pot of coffee was brought from the kitchen, and Beckworth poured for all three of them. Colonel Williams offered to have a cook rustle up some food, but Fargo declined. He had tasted army fare before.

"Well then, to business," Colonel Williams went on. "Captain Beckworth has told me that you once lived among the Sioux. Is this true?"

"Yes," Fargo confirmed. He felt no need to mention that it had been a long time ago, and that many of the skills for which he was noted stemmed in large measure from the teachings the Sioux had imparted.

The colonel was immensely pleased. "Then you are in a unique position to do this nation an invaluable service. The lives of countless innocent homesteaders rest on the decision you make here today."

Fargo took a sip of piping hot coffee while waiting for the commanding officer to get to the point.

"As you might know, we're sitting on a powder keg," Williams detailed. "It's our job to make sure the Winnebago stay on their reservation, and to protect the settlements in this region from the Chippewa and the Sioux, who have been giving us a great deal of trouble in recent months. Particularly the Sioux. I'm desperately afraid that the smallest incident will set them off, inciting a full-scale war."

"I don't see how I can be of any help," Fargo said when the man paused and regarded him expectantly. "You must have scouts on your payroll who are more familiar with the area than I am."

Colonel Williams made a teepee of his fingers. "Oh, yes, indeed we do. No, what I had in mind was for you to go talk to the Sioux. Calm their fears. Explain that if they make trouble, they will pay most dearly. That sort of thing."

The tin cup was suspended halfway to Fargo's mouth. "Do you have any idea what you're asking? Why should they listen to me?"

"You've lived with them—" Colonel Williams began.

"With the Tetons, who live hundreds of miles away on the plains," Fargo cut him off. "The Sioux who live here are the Santees. They don't know me from Adam. My word would carry no weight."

Both officers frowned. "But we had such high hopes," Captain Beckworth said, and leaned forward so none of the mess staff could overhear. "You see, Skye, we have reason to suspect that an unknown party is supplying guns to the Santees. With your help, maybe we can put a stop to it."

Just then the same orderly bustled up to the table and addressed the colonel. "Sir! Sorry to disturb you, but Lieutenant Miles urgently requests your presence outside right away. A civilian is causing a disturbance."

"Is that so?" Williams huffed, donning his hat. "Well, whoever it is will soon regret their mistake. Come along, Captain."

Out of curiosity, and to stretch his legs, Fargo trailed them, taking his coffee along. Yells and curses fell on his ears as he strolled through the doorway. That was when he saw Wagon Annie scattering troopers right and left with her bullwhip. Flabbergasted, he stopped—and the tip of the whip streaked toward his face.

SIGNET

THE WILD FRONTIER

☐ **JUSTIS COLT by Don Bendell.** The Colt Family Saga continues, with the danger, passion, and adventure of the American West. When Texas Ranger Justis Colt is ambushed by a gang of murderers, a mysterious stranger, Tora, saves his life. But now the motley crew of outlaws demand revenge and kill Tora's wife and two sons. Vengeance becomes a double-edged sword as Colt and Tora face the challenge of hunting down the killers. (182421—$4.99)

☐ **THE KILLING SEASON by Ralph Compton.** It was the 1870s—and the West was at its wildest. One man rode like a legend of death on this untamed frontier. His name was Nathan Stone, and he has learned to kill on the vengeance trail. He would have stopped after settling the score with his parents' savage slayers. But when you are the greatest gunfighter of all, there is no peace or resting place... (187873—$5.99)

☐ **THE HOMESMAN by Glendon Swarthout.** Briggs was an army deserter and claim jumper who was as low as a man could get. Mary Bee Cuddy was a spinster homesteader who acted like she was as good as any man. Together they had to take back east four women who had gone out of their minds and out of control. "An epic journey across the plains . . . as good as novels get."—*Cleveland Plain Dealer* (190319—$5.99)

*Prices slightly higher in Canada

Buy them at your local bookstore or use this convenient coupon for ordering.

PENGUIN USA
P.O. Box 999 — Dept. #17109
Bergenfield, New Jersey 07621

Please send me the books I have checked above.
I am enclosing $________________ (please add $2.00 to cover postage and handling). Send check or money order (no cash or C.O.D.'s) or charge by Mastercard or VISA (with a $15.00 minimum). Prices and numbers are subject to change without notice.

Card #______________________________ Exp. Date ____________________
Signature____
Name____
Address____
City ____________________ State ______________ Zip Code ______________

For faster service when ordering by credit card call **1-800-253-6476**

Allow a minimum of 4-6 weeks for delivery. This offer is subject to change without notice.